Asur Kanya & Her Route to Unrequited Love

By MVG (Maneesha Agrawal)

Invincible Publishers

First published in India in 2018

ISBN: 978-93-88333-20-7

Invincible Publishers

G-120, Sushant Lok III, Sector 57, Gurgaon-122002

Registered Address: Opposite Kasturba Ashram, Radaur, Haryana–135133

Printed at Thomson Press (India) LTD

DEDICATED TO
SH. VIVEK GUPTA

Acknowledgement

Mahakavi Jaishanker Prasad, who immortalized Manu, Ira and Shradhha in his great work **'KAMAYANI'**

Perched on the bough of a very dark night,
were a pair of eyes penetrating their sight
into the realm of the years gone by
scouring the pathway for morning at nigh.....

ABOUT THE AUTHOR

MVG (Maneesha Agrawal) is the author of this book, this being her second published work. Her first book, 'From Zero To One – the story of Manu' was well received by readers and has earned rave reviews from amongst the readers and critics both. It was based on the story of Manu - a tale travelling since timeworn ages surpassing all the boundaries of country, region and religion.

The first book's success was an achievement and it delivered the author an acceptance with the readers as a singular writer, who presented rationalized fiction (based on researched facts) spun around captivating folklore. Response to the aforesaid title was fairly mentionable even at the prestigious World Book Fair Feb'2017, held at Pragati Maidan, New Delhi where the book 'From Zero To One' sold over a hundred copies.

MVG is a writer driven by an honesty in her perception. Her incredible knowledge of ancient Indian history which she has garnered through her reading preferences gets clearly manifested in her work. She has a knack dealing with the past, shuffling through the sheets of unfamiliar chronicles – an eminence that has now encouraged her to write this second book.

Ms. Maneesha is a widely travelled voyager, with a penchant for exploring pieces of history shroud under the wraps of time slumbering at strange, obscure places. It has often led her to discovering new faces and facets of tales told and retold since centuries. This is her passion, of knowing the unknown and creating fiction around facts that binds the two together….in an irresistible narrative! Read on to believe!

FOREWORD FROM THE AUTHOR

Love – a sentiment, a devotion, an ecstasy, a sanctity. So much has been said and written about it since time immemorial that one tends to think there's nothing more left to be added. But it has always surprised the thinkers and the writers alike when strange, unexplored episodes are found unfolding every time its domain is reached. So while the variance is quite expected, the manifestations of love is and shall continue to remain a subject for more exploration.

We are living in a 'blink-and-you-missed the emotion' age. But if the frenzied human race of current times could stop for a while and consider the coarseness with which we usually deal with love - the sanctimonious sentiment we might see how we are getting it all wrong.

It is a sentiment – not an emotion which many of us are making it out to be. When I say this, I should like to elaborate a bit more on the difference the two terms denote.

Sentiment from what I understand is the verve of an alive heart. It stays with the core, as the innate spirit and strength of a person's character. It does not change or alter with neither time nor situation. Although sometimes it may fade away from the visible horizon or even be oblivious, laying passive under the twirl of twisting circumstances but it is there for sure –

steadfastly providing essential vitality for the life to go on.

Emotion on the other hand is a passing upsurge, which surfaces as the result of some overriding persuasion of a particular sentiment. It is bound to appear and go, sooner or maybe sometimes later. It cannot sustain after the sentiment that had stirred it gets kerbed by the controlling power of brain. It is transient, and can never stay forever.

Rage, laughter, twinge, hunger, lust....all are emotions not to be confused as sentiments. But we often mix the two, not realizing the difference between desire and hunger, pain and pang, anger and rage, love and lust. This confused mixing leads to complex mazes we end up creating for ourselves like the way Ira, the principal character of the story here does.

Now Ira is a character whom any of the modern day girls can easily relate to. She is an independent thinker, a girl fully aware of her rights and preferences.

She doesn't like to get hassled – refusing to succumb to the do's and don'ts of the so called prevalent social systems. She likes to enjoy life liberally in her own sweet way. Her endearing character however, undergoes a startling transformation when she starts getting played upon by her own emotional fixations. How and where she went wrong within her naïve imperfection is what makes the rest of the story.

The story of Ira, Manu and Kamayani is indicated in a few of the ancient Sanskrit texts. Using these only available outlines (which I could gather bit by bit from our age old Sanskrit scriptures) as the framework for my story I have tried my best not to exceed any margins, especially in moulding the characters and their indulgences. The incidents and entities used into the chronicle are also in close proximity to their original write-ups as appearing in the ancient books. I must admit that was some real hard work.

A very intellectual configuration to this very same story is provided by ***Mahakavi Jai Shankar Prasad,*** the harbinger of Hindi Literature, in his masterpiece "***Kamayani***".

There, the three principal characters are treated as figurative metaphors... Manu symbolizing the eternal soul committed to create, Kamayani as the sanctified sentiment that provides core strength, and Ira is symbolic of mind's unstable diversions. It is written in a ballad form, beautifully utilizing live characters as metaphors to define the complex occupations of heart, mind and soul (as Kamayani, Ira and Manu in that order).

Every time I have read '***Kamayani***' I have found something new – a fresh outlook on the way these three entities have to struggle within their ambit. But sometimes they must get congealed to create the substantial. This book is also a tribute to Sh. Jai Shankar Prasad's extraordinary conceptualization.

As an afterthought I can say that I may or may not have succeeded in enhancing the splendour of this already impressive chronicle stacked in some obscure ledges of history - but I strongly believe in the authenticity of the characters that I present here, who I trust did exist in some bracket of history that our civilization has travelled through.

With a wish to be read enjoyably by generous readers,

MVG (Maneesha Agrawal)

Note:

My first book, 'From Zero To One – the story of Manu' had dealt with a certain tale of massive floods occurring across the globe that had wiped off majority of human population from the Earth's surface thousands of years ago. There was only one survivor left, Manu. He had initiated a fresh start for the civilization – this is a story which finds place in almost all the ancient religious texts as well as available history books.

This link from the first book is utilized here. But the continuity of characters, places and incidents is carefully handled so as to keep the inter-dependence of the two stories completely unaffected. The munificent readers who have this book in their hands (but haven't read FZTO) have an equal right to enjoy reading as those kind readers who have already read and appreciated my first book.

Also for those looking for history I have a bit of striking information to share. **The Causeruman mountain range which makes the setting for this particular story is none other than the famous Caucasus Mountain of today. They have a mention in our Puranas as Causeruman or Chas Giri. The early nineteenth century British traveller Captain Francis Wilford has written at length about this region's Vedic links. Apparently there have been reasons to believe that the people living in that part of the world had some day, some basic root connections with the Indian civilization. During my**

research for this book I have come across certain evidences that strongly indicate such a connection.

But I refrain from delving further into the survey here and as an author I acknowledge my story as a work of fiction not based on certified facts.

SECTION I

ANOTHER BEGINNING

CHAPTER 1
A NEW STORY

Banasur travelled up north of Himalayan ranges. What he was in pursuit of he did not stop to think.

He let his feet lead him to a realm where he could be more like himself – the erstwhile Asur King Banasur, mean and atrocious Banasur. He felt the need to get away from everything including every miserable soul who had spoiled his more recent past – the Manavas, Yakshas, Adityas, and Manu[1].

After wandering aimlessly for about more than a couple of months in the hostile rockery he unknowingly reached the higher Causeruman[2] range lying west of the great Himalayas.

He was dejected and forlorn, but not defeated. His arrogance had upheld the determination with which he had survived the great deluge[3] – the determination to find a world of his own someday. His tired and weary eyes had searched every horizon and explored every landscape to look for some purpose or place which he could associate himself with. And one day finally they were rewarded,

---

[1] The first king of human civilization, Book ref. 'From Zero To One – The Story Of Manu' by MVG (Maneesha Agrawal)

[2] The Caucasus Mountains

[3] The great floods occurring thousands of years ago, Book ref. 'From Zero To One – The Story Of Manu' by MVG (Maneesha Agrawal)

"My strength be my soul!" he said to himself, "That stone structure looks like bastions of the fabled stone castle of the great King Shambarasur[4]! Of course it is, for no other such castle exists anywhere else on this earth. This means I could be in the Causeruman range, the ideal place my destiny has brought me to".

With a revived hope Banasur quickened his steps to reach the impervious looking gates of a startling stone castle.

[4] A famous Asur (one of the undomesticated, undisciplined tribes of Vedic era) King known to have built 100 stone castles.

CHAPTER 2
A PROPOSAL

I

Ira sat contemplating the proposal. Her thick and long eyelashes lounged over her honey-dew cheeks that contoured her beautifully round face. She was thinking. Her golden locks kept straying around that pensive pretence as if struggling to search for an answer. Nadia, Ira's maid (and also a close friend) stood watching her quietly before she finally said,

"What is there to think so hard? You are merely asked to consider - mind you - just consider having Banasur as your partner at the Sammon[5] tonight. You can simply say a 'yes' or a 'no' for this. Why won't you?"

Ira lifted her pretty head from her palm and opened her large sapphire blue eyes,

"Yes I must, and that is exactly where my difficulty lies. I do not have iota of an intention to say yes to the proposal. Heaven knows why but I have always felt a strong aversion to that fellow's intolerable snobbery....which I know is there! No matter how well he behaves, or how loyally he's won combats for us, or how quickly he's become father's right hand man within two years...I still despise him if I may use the word."

---

[5] A festival (celebrated at some places only) of pre-Vedic times, somewhat like a modern day carnival

"Okay. Then just say so to your father." Nadia shrugged her shoulders with a disapproving head-shake.

"Nope…I think it will be harsh on father as I do not have a reason to refuse. So maybe, just to honour his word I shall go to the carnival with Banasur…and who knows tonight's excursion will equip me with a reason to say no. What do you suggest?"

"Well as you think, it might work or it might also work the other way," said Nadia lowering her tone down for the latter part of the sentence.

"You mean I will change my opinion about him? That's not happening. Even if I fail to see a reason I will never like him. Never! Because I do hate him, really!" she said stamping her foot hard on ground.

"Oh whatever!" Nadia released her argument, "Now since you are going to the carnival tonight I suggest that you get up and change into some better drapery. Otherwise you are going to blame it on me for not reminding you in time."

Quite so, thought Ira and proceeded to her changing room. She shuffled through her colourful draperies (mostly loose fitted gowns and stoles) and selected a pale green dress which though worn out was still an impressive outfit. She didn't want to wear something new and exclusive, for she wanted Banasur not to have his eyes glued to her.

Having done her hair and the dressing Nadia scrutinized her work from different angles murmuring,

"I have no clue on how to make you look unattractive....you will be arresting all eyes even in worse rugs!"

"Come now, Nadia. I think you are overdoing it. At least let me have a hope alive – that fellow himself declining to make a match with me after seeing me in such a weird grab!" Ira was irritated. She disliked the idea of being alongside Banasur and so her temper had flared up unreasonably this time.

"Declining indeed!" arching her brows Nadia left her alone.

II

Shambarasur was a powerful king in the region. He had been the army commander for an erstwhile Asur kingdom near Saurashtra[6]. He was forced to flee his homeland after facing defeat in a decisive battle Asuras fought years ago against their arch-rivals, the Adityas[7]. His life was saved, and some of his men had also survived.

Thereafter starting anew with leading a small group which grew in due course joined by few more huntsmen who came together searching for food and shelter in the region decades ago he had reached the current status through his grit, wits and guts. He was rough, shrewd, ruthless and cunning when he was a warrior and he was lenient, spirited, jovial and carefree when he was a king. He never believed in laws – and didn't expect his

---

[6] Modern day Gujrat

[7] One of the most powerful Vedic clans

subjects to follow any either. As a result, he ruled a set of unruly people who did not conform to any discipline or order of any kind.

Regulations were absent, and the society was astray. But since they were a naturally strong population living in one of the toughest terrain of Causeruman, Shambarasur's men were well capable of living in their own way – lawlessly, haphazardly with their self-fancied rubrics. They were used to guarding their personal interests in their own fashion.

Nothing worried them, for they feared none.

The wild subjects of Cuseru, as the region was called, lived to make merry each day. They had no use for anything called intellect albeit their strong hands were skilled in a wide range of arts, crafts and construction. Their cerebral working touched the floor but their physical strength was indomitable which they aptly used in creating ambitious structures. The gigantic stone fortress they had built for themselves was one such impressive example of the magnificent Asur craftsmanship.

The Asuras cultivated negligibly by tilling the land and were quite happy devouring milk and meat of available animals whom they reared for the purpose. Honey, dried fruits and alcohol were the other savouries their society was fond of. Such were the rowdy Asuras - a wild populace driven only by desires and fancies.

III

The eccentric Asuras of Causeruman had contrived of some curious traditions and festivals for celebrating life. They had devised Sammon, a week long yearly carnival to commemorate their King's first victory over the region's native people – the erstwhile residents of Cuseru.

Before Shambar and his men entered the territory a village Cuseru was thriving in the region. The people lived peacefully without a king and an army. They flourished within a community regulated regime.

These original Cuseruans were believed to have branched out from the people of Bramhavart[8] ages ago. They had been living in the terrain since time immemorial until when a few decades ago they were defeated, enslaved and almost eliminated by the Shambarasur reign. His militancy had turned the otherwise peaceful region into an aggressive, disorderly and feral zone.

The Asur folks had looted and hacked the villagers mercilessly sparing only the ones whom they found physically unfit and mentally slow, fit to serve their captors – Shambar's men. Resultantly the original Cuseruan culture and creed was completely eradicated along with the majority of its native population.

Nadia, the companion to Ira was one such Cuseruan survivor. She had survived the Asur invasion as a very small kid hiding behind her grandmother's dead body.

---

[8] The northern region of India, extending from Afghanistan to China in the north

King Shambarasur had spotted the girl and was taken in by her small, intelligent eyes even at that young age. The fact that she wasn't crying amid that violent sight had struck the hardened invader favourably and he had lifted the child upon his instinct. He had liked her, thinking of an important role for her.

Nadia obviously could not remember anything from her childhood except for a Granny who told her stories from the great land of Bramhavart. Plain but austere to look at she had inherited the sharp, analytical brain of original Cuseruan race. Her straight black hair were always plaited and wound around her square face, and her beady black eyes were always alert. She wasn't exactly pretty, but smart…as if having an intelligent authority at her command.

The original Cuseruan society was actually in many ways (including the physical features to some extent) similar to their ancestors from Bramhavart. But who could have known anything about them now… as most of them were already dead. And the ones who lived, didn't have the capability to be served by their memory correctly including our good Nadia.

Nadia grew up knowing Ira as the lone friend, family, or relation she could see around. Noticing her dedication Shambar had been exceptionally nice to her assigning her his motherless daughter's close company.

Thus entrusted the custody of the Princess, Nadia was raised as adequately as was Ira. She was taught and brought up under the same supervision as was the Princess. Shambar could have no fear of any attempt to revenge-seeking from her side, for her family was dead and the handful of remaining Cuseruan community members were all loyal slaves to the Asuras now.

IV

At the Sammon festival the unruly Asuras made merry. There were held savage animal races, grotesque duels, warfare competitions, violent drinking and dancing, some interesting bazaars and everything else one could think of. Here everything was open for everyone's enjoyment. It really looked more like a brash extravagance... of some disfigured vitality of life.

Nevertheless, there were some enjoyable additions too. One such exciting feature of the carnival was the 'Vayas' tradition. It was an event where men were given a chance to win over the fairer gender in a unique way that was re-invented every year, to keep the excitement raised.

This particular year it was decided that a man who wanted a particular girl or a lady, should plant a fig twig in the backyard of her dwelling without being seen by anyone at all. If the man could manage, the girl or the lady had no choice but to concede to his desires... But if caught, he was to receive a twig bashing from all the ladies who were gladly waiting to do the services!

This and many more bizarrely interesting customs were introduced every year by the disorderly, rowdy Asuras. But such was their way to enjoy life...which they certainly did to the hilt.

The man-animal races and combative duels were their worst enjoyment. These contests were not at all pleasant to look at and a lot of bloody, gory scenes were often staged. But from the Asur perspective beholding or participating in such grisliness were the hallmarks of nerve and gallantry. Their crowds cheered at such events in maximum strengths, prompting the participants to be more and more severe.

Such sequences, naturally ended with a few lives kaput in the vilest possible way.

Even in the women folk where a softer heart is expected to be present, aversion to those appalling scenes was surprisingly absent…with barely a few exceptions. Ira was one of them.

She loathed being a part of the crowds watching the gruesome, barbaric rivalries. Her stubborn but gentle heart revolted against the cruel exuberance of her savage tribe. Probably it was her genes (from the maternal side) that made her think differently. She could not like any of those brutes, never!

V

Ira was the prize Banasur wanted for his services to Shambar. His rough and rugged face attained surprisingly mellowed miens whenever she was around. His manner changed from being pompous to propitiatory…at the sight of her. How many times he had wished to have his impact on her. But apparently up-till now, he couldn't have any. Ira would not even look at him...not even a remote disinterested look. She clearly ignored him quite high-handedly, he had felt.

Banasur was supercilious but he too had a heart which was craving for a desire – a desire for love, for the warmth of his own home and hearth. He had left far behind his country, his people, and every memory of whatever he'd owned back then.

He now wanted to make his home here at Causeruman ... with Ira. He was waiting for his chance to take up the issue directly with Shambar. After all who was there to deserve Ira more than him?

As the Sammon approached that year, Shambar himself asked Bana to take his daughter to the carnival for company.

The Asur-king was contemplating Ira-Bana match for some time now, and he had already noticed Banasur's attentive glances at his daughter. Things couldn't be better for either of them since each of the two Asuras (Shambar and Bana) were thinking about the alliance being the best proposition for further carrying on the Asur lineage. The king, however was alienated on his daughter's aversion to the person he had chosen for her.

CHAPTER 3

AT THE SAMMONS

I

Ira moved around at the Carnival with Banasur walking by her side. He made sheepish glances at her beautiful radiant face and an occasional brushing of the floating greenery of her dress made his heart whack louder within his ribs. He was faltering, but trying very hard to get her enter into a conversation evidently without much success.

Ira remained remote. Her aficionado's attempts had appeared more and more boisterous to her. Bana, soon tired of trying looked around to search for some really interesting event that could capture his companion's attention.

The couple roamed aimlessly into the setting and abruptly entered a scene of an Asur v/s bull fight.

An enormous bull was raging at its opponent, an equally horrific Asur with swollen reddened eyes waiting to grab the animal by its antlers. There were many by-standers who were enjoying the act... swearing and challenging at the two growling fighters.

The Asur[9] in Bana got charged up and he forgot the obligatory disciplines for the immaculate company he was privileged to have that evening. He grunted and

[9] Literal meaning "savage" in Sanskrit

yelled at the bull, and swerving his arms excitedly at the two combatants waded through the crowds to reach close to the fighting rink. His gang (subordinates – he was the chief army commander) who was already there joined him and soon they all were a part of that horrific surge of savage hollers!

Ira was already worked up with Banasur's inadequate mannerisms. The man didn't seem to have any brains. All he could do was growl and brawl… how awfully revolting it was to be sharing even one evening with him! And to think of a whole life….! Never.

She was looking for an escape and Bana's horrifying antics gave her just the right trice. She slipped out of the scene before she could be made to witness the bloody battle of two fuming beasts.

The Princess wandered around aimlessly, searching for a distraction from the incongruous company she had just deserted. Her eyes rested at a small shack selling beads and stones. Distractedly she lifted a few in her palm and ran her fingers through them,

"Do take them, my pretty princess," said the old woman at the shop, "they won't cost you much".

"Hmm? ...yes, maybe I'll like them", Ira replied.

"Oh yes you will like them, my princess. These are rare Himalayan stones….not found in this region. They are known for their brilliance. My son has to go very far off to Himalayas to collect them…takes him about a month to bring such delicacies…you won't find them elsewhere. Here, see these", she extended a handful of coloured shining stones at the princess who took them in her rosy palms. They were glittering, and Ira was staring at them still absent-mindedly.

"Ooo....these are really good!" exclaimed Nadia from over Ira's shoulder.

"You! .....how you scared me! What are you doing here?" Ira was startled.

"Banasur came to me searching for you. And I had an idea where you could be found. But my dear girl, why did you have to ditch him in the first place?"

"I was wearied. I couldn't continue...to torture myself. Oh...I was so...so..."

"What is it Ira? You look distraught. He err....he didn't offend you, did he?"

"Nah! Not that. But I am appalled... at the mere idea. Nadia, I don't want to talk about him now. See these lovely Himalayan stones...I think I like them. I do. I actually want them."

"O...okay. We can talk about such things later. Yes, even I think these stones are brilliant – why, that large pink one can be worn in a neckpiece and.....umm....these are more suitable for earrings....or why not...."

Nadia was a real treasure for Ira. She knew Ira's mood swings so well and also had the correct approach to handle them. Her broad face seldom showed up a wrinkle signifying her patience and her controlled eloquence. This was a very essential feature required for

Ira's companionship because the royal girl sometimes played a thorough brat! She was prone to having her streaks oscillate.

The two girls shopped at the Sammon with an absolute memory loss on the evening's burning issue, Banasur. They bought Himalayan gems, clothes, masonry artefacts and whatever attracted them.

II

Morning at the stone castle arrived with Bana approaching Shambarasur for a serious dialogue. He wanted to have complete clarity on what future his dream-girl and his king had decided for him. 'I've had enough of self-speculations and attentive tomfoolery', he had been thinking after yesterday's episode.

Shambar quietly listened to Bana's words which were more of a questioning nature rather than grumbling. Banasur was wise enough to know how adoringly the King loved his only child. No one dared complain to her father on her conduct!

Shambar sighed and signalled Bana to wait while he called his daughter to his chamber.

Ira came alone, intrepidly yet with a shade apprehensively. The King addressed the two across each other,

"Ira," he said, "I always thought you and Bana were nicely suited to make a match for each other. You are the only descendent I have and Bana is my most worthy greenhorn. My dear girl, you already know that the one whom you will marry is going to be our next King. I have pitched in so much for both of you as a parent as well as a King. But…"

Shambar looked at his daughter for a moment and continued, "…. after yesterday evening I am bound to think that I may have been wrong. You, Ira, for some strange reason seem to refuse to accept this tie-up. So I have called you to hear from you what exactly your thoughts are in this regard. Open up, child…for I am your father and the King here to listen to your will and fulfil your wish."

Ira stood there listening to her father's stoic observations.

It was now for her to decide and speak up. She had also been thinking the whole night. Her inner consciousness had asked her several times….what was it that she wanted? What would she choose for herself? Did she like being the future queen of Asuras? Did she want to be married to one of those ferocious fiends (that is how she always thought of the Asuras) … further carrying their legacy and lineage? Will she be happy, restricting herself to this space?

No. She wanted to see the world independently. She wanted to explore her options. She lay awake dreaming of a more civil society, better, nicer people - the ones whom she would care for… emotionally attach with… and probably, love. And maybe she would even live as a part of a better civilization someday. She could not contribute to or be subjected to this savageness for the rest of her whole life. She could not marry someone within her own society, she saw it more clearly than ever. But presently she only said,

"Father, even I have thought about it very sincerely last night. And I must confess that I do not want to marry Banasur. I mean not right now. No…it is not because I have something against him particularly…. he might actually be a really nice, good fellow", Ira eyed Banasur who stood blinking coyly, "I'm sure he is good. But father, I do not want to marry right now. I want to see more of this world, travel to places other than the Causeruman, meet different people and explore varied cultures. I want to know many other things that are happening under the sun!"

"….know other things happening under the sun? What do you mean by this? Ira, are you serious?" Shambar was baffled.

"Oh father! How do I explain…I…I feel I have a calling from some farther lands which I've never seen and never heard of. I've often dreamt of some remote territory that sits pretty… maybe far away from our Causeruman. A place where the winds sing and petals dance, the sun shines showering exceptional warmth, flowers bloom and the waters lie unruffled… Oh…! I am putting it very badly father, for I cannot point out what is it that I want. But I think I do know one thing. I shall not be happy entering into a marriage before I can satiate this… this strange yearning."

"Hmm... strange yearning."

"I have to do it once, father. I must. Because I know....I am not going to be happy ever if you ask me to stay confined to our Causeruman. For one, I want to see the world on my own. And two, I will be able to decide what I want out of life only if I am left to myself." Ira stressed.

Shambar sat quiet rubbing his chin with his hand. He loved his only daughter and wanted all the happiness for her. Ira's mother had died the day the girl was born. She was, some people believed, a village belle from some region near Bramhavart who was forcibly abducted and married to by Shambar during one of his stormy conquests. That was Shambar's only romantic infatuation he ever had. He never married again, content with having Ira as his only daughter whom he loved more than anything. And he was aware of her inheritance – beauty and kindness from her mother's side and an obdurate resolve from her father's.

Theirs was an open society completely out of bounds. He could not impose his choices upon Ira forcibly. The Asuras had never lived under any social, moral or cultural pressure ever since they were flourishing. When each member of their populace had the liberty to pursue personal inclinations in each matter, then so had Ira.

And of course she was not the one who could be coerced or forced into a thing as serious as marriage...nah, not her! He thought for a while and lifted his head as the other two waited silently for his response,

"Your wanderlust, for I prefer to call it that only, is a thing which you get genetically transferred – from me. I had this same craving in my frame that had landed me here years ago. I know how strong and unsettling it is…. but there it is and nothing can be done about it. Now you, Ira, are the future of this Kingdom and you have certain onuses. Whatever you do is going to impact the whole lot... so you need to be careful with your decisions and deeds. In my opinion all…… or eh Banasur, what do you have to say?" Shambar said suddenly remembering the presence of Bana and turning to him for advice.

"I….Me? What is there for me to say?" Banasur mumbled and looked blandly at the pretty face of Ira.

"I protest! It's about me, so I must have a say first, father!" Ira protested clenching her fists and stamping her feet.

The King retreated, "Ah….Okay. Alright. We are Asuras…. out of all bounds. We do not believe in forcing decisions. And even if I did, the Asur trait in my blood is going to revolt… how well I know my blood! Ira, you will not marry Bana unless you've had your chance and your choice. Is that so?"

She signalled tilting her head in affirmative. She was frowning at the undue importance her father had just now given to that foolish Banasur.

"Very well then. Let us decide on something here. I will permit Ira to have a complete twelve months of drifting and travelling at her own will. We shall let her go, and let her explore the world with her open eyes and free mind. But remember Ira after this one year you must come home to us – to me, to Causeruman and probably Banasur, if he is ready to wait for you till that time."

"I will wait, my dear King I will wait. I can wait for her as long as she asks me to. I will gladly wait for my lady luck to smile at me after another twelve months. I am already so much indebted to you and your kindly people.....and what after all, is a twelve months time – just a one year! It is nothing in comparison with the regard I have for you and your daughter. I am quite okay really...quite prepared." Banasur was quick to express his modesty and loyalty.

His hope of having Ira was revived once again after Shambar had fixed the time frame for her. Bana knew that she was less likely to find any social set-up elsewhere owing to the wash out world had seen during the great floods[10]. 'No harm in letting her roam about a bit', he had thought.

The only part which he knew was inhabited, was Manali and Malana[11] in the higher Himalayan range. It was an unapproachable region for the delicate Asur princess to travel to.... She may never even come to know that they existed. Thus feeling safe he was willing to show-off his liberality and loyalty at this delicate moment which was currently being seen as one of the most disciplined scene ever at Shambar's stone castle.

---

[10] The great floods occurring thousands of years ago, Book ref. 'From Zero To One – The Story Of Manu' by MVG (Maneesha Agrawal)

[11] Book ref. 'From Zero To One – The Story Of Manu' by MVG (Maneesha Agrawal)

Judging the requirement of a display of solidarity towards her father the princess also responded, "I also promise to do everything you would want me to once I am back."

"So when do you propose to leave?" the father asked.

"Ah…well, why not tomorrow if I may?" Ira replied.

"Very well then. I will depute Damanasur and his ten armed men to go along with you and Nadia. The caravan shall get ready before evening tonight for me to inspect. An adequate reserve of food, medicine and arms shall accompany you. Five of your maids and five servants are also travelling with you, before you start protesting against my arrangements!" Shambar had already eyed knitting of his daughter's brows and twitching of her lips. He continued without giving her a chance to interrupt,

"Banasur, do you think Damas (Damanasur) is suitable to carry out the responsibility?"

"Certainly my King. Damas is our best and most trustworthy man. You have made an excellent choice. I myself would have liked to accompany the princess but for her willingness. Yet Damas is going to be good." added Bana, covertly eyeing the pretty princess.

CHAPTER 4

IRA'S CARAVAN

I

Ira and Nadia were tired. Their caravan had been travelling for months now. They had crossed the Causeruman kingdom, slowly descending down to the mild and un-agitated waters of the Cashyap[12] Sea. Then tilting their compass eastwards as per the Princess's wish (in pursuit of Himalayas, probably) they had continued travelling to east.

The group had been happy at the start of their unconventional journey. They were delighted at the sight of colourful flora and variant water hues of many unknown rivers and water bodies they had crossed – everything had looked so wonderful! Every scenery, each sight was so atypical of what they had ever seen at their rough and rugged Causeruman.

They had enjoyed traversing through the beautiful vast plains of Sindhu[13] and rejoiced scaling the effervescent low lying banks of a sparkling Saraswati[14]. Nature was so brilliant all over the world… Beyond the confines of kingdoms and palaces it's unregimented beauty and essence was spellbinding! Everything was oh so charming.

---

[12] Vedic era name for the present day Caspian Sea

[13] Modern day Indus

[14] A Vedic Era river, now extinct

But no civilization, no society was to be found anywhere on their route. The great floods[15] had extensively eliminated all life forms in the zone and except for a few winged wanderers, no one appeared on or beyond the weathered horizon. The Causeruman Caravan was yet to find a civilization, a habitat, or a trace of fellow human beings. Roaming about for nearly six months our enthusiastic travellers were tired now.

"Ira, what have we been doing all these months…we have seen enough of this bright glowing landscape and beautiful scenery. I think we can always go back even before the twelve months are over." Nadia suggested, trying to be more realistic.

"….."

"Ira, what are you thinking?"

"Himalayas."

"Himalayas…. the Eastern Mountains? What of it?"

"I want to see the Himalayas. You remember that bead seller….the way she was talking about Himalayas. It's got beautiful stones and some of the most precious treasures. It is in the land of Aaryavart[16]. We've heard such interesting stories about the people of Aaryavart from our nanny in childhood, you remember? Even you said your granny told you some. I think it would be a nice, fascinating region….you know it has always attracted me ever since I heard the name in our

[15] Ref : book - From Zero To One, the story of Manu by MVG (Maneesha Agrawal)

[16] The whole of Indian region. In Vedic times it was believed to be spanning west to east from the gulf till china in the north and till Sri Lanka in the south.

childhood. I have thought much about that land - the beautiful culture and the people there… and I've often…. (– often dreamt of a prince from Aaryavart marrying me, she had said to herself). So why not let's go there?"

"Okay. To Himalayas then". Naturally Nadia couldn't suspect.

II

Damanasur or Damas as he was known was leading a small Caravan to the magnificent Himalayas. He crossed the rocky hills, scaled the invincible territory and was soon set to enter the region of Manavas[17] through the entry gate to Aaryavart which was the Rohtang Pass[18]. Damas was a very quiet and obedient marshal who could refrain from asking un-authorized questions from his Masters.

After having assigned a commission he seldom used to think why the particular order was issued to him. Exploring Aaryavart was something his Masters wanted, so he would do it at any cost. Such was his infallible loyalty towards the Royal traveller.

III

It was a spring summer morning. The small Caravan from Causeruman landed at this region of the planet for the first time. It wasn't snowing and they quite easily

---

[17] The followers of Manu (ref : book - From Zero To One, the story of Manu by MVG Maneesha Agrawal))

[18] Rohtang Pass in Himalayas provides entry into India to travellers coming from Afghanistan side. It opens up onto the region of Manali.

made way for a levelled and comfortable ground to repose for a few days, which they soon found close by a serene river. It was none other than our familiar Arjikiya[19]. They raised a pavilion on the placid banks of Arjikiya.

The evening assembled slowly and the Asur Princess looked around.....

An auburn sun was trying to re-colour

the resplendent waters that already wore

shades of marvel

waves did explore.

A glistening blue strewn up so high.....

Few winged seraphs crooned

at the radiance of the colourful bloom

the earth adorned under that sky.

The air bore scent,

playing with thy

stiller strands and their verve

brushing them dry....!

Was this heaven?

"Oh Nadia....Nadia! Can the world be so beautiful? Look at these tiny birds, the resplendent flowers, the

[19] Older (vedic) name for river Vipasha, Vyaas or modern day Beas – Ref – 'From Zero To One – by MVG (Maneesha Agrawal)'

scented air and cheerful waters! This is so beautiful…heavenly. I…I can live here for ages!" Ira was whirling with the wind spreading her arms out like a child in ecstasy.

"I'm sure you can. But you won't. It is really beautiful and lively here I agree….but one's own motherland always calls you back," said the cold companion. She had a very practical brain and seldom only succumbed to the callings of heart. Her vigilant sense of responsibility always overcame her emotions and for this reason she was trusted by Shambar as the ideal companion to his dear daughter.

"Ah for once Nadia! Forget about everything else! Can't you feel the warmth of this gracious sun, this forthcoming land…this welcoming sky? Feel it once Nadia, and just forget about everything else." Ira looked at her friend's impassive face. But she had merely shrugged her straight, broad shoulders.

"Oh! Can you ever feel an attraction?"

"Indeed I will, some day when I'm dead." said Nadia raising her eyebrows and left the Princess alone with her exuberant spirits.

Nadia had a stronger head than heart which resented the idea of surrendering to a fanciful desire.

Looking at her determined, angular face no one could actually imagine Nadia succumbing to the aspirations and emotions of heart. She could never fall in love - Ira had often thought. The idea of never seeing a dream, never nourishing a desire and never pursuing a fantasy made her think very pitiably of Nadia… But then of course what a wise girl she was, when it came to do some intelligent thinking.

Nadia left as she had to work for arranging a lot many things since the Caravan intended to stay put for a few weeks or maybe more, looking at the Princess's penchants. Ira and her crew settled at the banks of Arjikiya without having any idea of the place's significance.

It were the outskirts of village Manali, the first habitat of Manavas[20] – the followers of our civilization's first King Manu[21].

---

[20] Literal meaning the followers of Manu

[21] Book Ref. 'From Zero To One – The Story Of Manu' by MVG (Maneesha Agrawal)

SECTION II

A NEW TANGENT

CHAPTER 5

MANALI[22]

I

Village Manali was prospering. It was the initial refuge for Manu and Manavas, but had now flourished into quite an animated village bustling with life over these few years. The dwellers of Manali were advancing as a competent society, healthy at heart and wealthy at resources. They had fought courageously against every odd and had now regained the mislaid splendour of their worthy lives. They were the hard-working, perceptive forbearers of a race which duly went on to advance as the modern day human race of scientific resurgence[23].

Son of King Surya of Bramhavart Shradhhdev[24] Manu was the first King of Manavas. He was their leader whom everyone looked up to. His astuteness saw the goals and his proficiency showed the way. His calibre got results and his influence carried his people. He was loved by all and he loved all. His magnetism had increased many folds since the early days of the group's struggle - so much so that it had now reached a divine status. Manavas were the following subjects and

---

[22] The land of Manu in Sanskrit (Manu + Sthali = Manu + Land), Modern day Manali

[23] Book ref. 'From Zero To One – The Story Of Manu' by MVG (Maneesha Agrawal)

[24] Manu's original name was Shradhhdev. He was called Manu as he was the most profound thinker (from Sanskrit word 'Manan' meaning 'to think')

King Manu, the best among all mortals was their heart mind and soul.

Kamayani was their Queen and an ideal consort to the King. She was of a highly admirable character with a distinct sense of her duties and responsibilities. The first Manav Queen was devoted as seen correctly by the wise Saptrishis[25] and did not disrupt the set-up never urging Manu to act her husband. She had anchored her husband's will and stance in each and every quest Manu had taken up.

The principal Manav couple had committed their lives to uplifting of their people's. To the extent that though married for a couple of years now they had observed celibacy till the time they thought their community had reached its zenith. Time was yet to come when the Manavas would see their spearheads start their journey to personal happiness – by being a man and wife.

Life at Manu-sthali[26], or Manali was gradually gaining affluence. The industrious Manavas were tilling the land and domesticating the cattle to their opulence. They were growing food grains, rich fruits and vegetables in ample quantities.

New findings were being added to the already rich knowledge scores they possessed. They were discovering new vistas for equipping their coming generations, enriching their expertise with a style they believed to be more suitable for celebrating life. They

---

[25] Seven famous Sages (Sapt + Rishi = Seven + Sages) of Vedic Era

[26] The land of Manu in Sanskrit (Manu + Sthali = Manu's + Land)

had developed useful crafts, making a noteworthy progress with the stimuli life had provided by giving a second chance to them. They were very happy, savouring their delight in the urbane way they lived.

The residents of Manali wore a variety of finely spun and woven clothes that were rolled out of their spinning wheels using fibres from cotton, silk and wool. The yarns were dyed in a range of colours and woven into exquisite drapery, sometimes embroidered with intricate borders of thread and bead-work.

The Manavas were ornamental by nature and their sophistications were classy. They adorned embellishments of gold and silver, tastefully crafted with inlay work of locally found precious gems, stones and pearls.

Their hamlet was neat and picturesque where homes were adequately furnished with all the comforts of living. This was a story that had begun well and was all set to make imprints for the future generations to follow.

II

The day had plunged, slowly descending down to its duskier half.

The first Manav King Manu returned to his chalet at the Boat Cliff[27] where Kamayani stood waiting for her soul's delight to come home. She saw him approaching at some distance and once again her pulse started racing faster. It always happened to her. Ever since he had held

[27] A Cliff where Manu is said to have tied his boat to after the famous floods - Book ref. 'From Zero To One – The Story Of Manu' by MVG (Maneesha Agrawal)

her hand for that first time on the Boat Cliff[28], she could never control her emotional trembles in his presence. How could she… Manu was enticement!

Her husband was mostly out on his calls, often not returning home being bound to his duties. His subjects had to search for newer soils and his team had to work on them turning the available patches into yielding farmlands. They were busy discussing and inventing new tools. They had to discover new techniques to proliferate their produce. They had to construct new irrigation channels to provide water to their expanding fields during dry season. They were to erect new structures and systems to exceed their initiations. They needed to consult their mentors Saptrishis and the wise Adityas to formulate their social evolution step by step.

All this required a fair bit of exploring and frequent travelling to far off places for their leader. As a result Manu was Kamayani's own Manu very rarely….and when he was, Kamayani wasn't herself!!

Today the Manav King had a comparatively smaller day and he had ample reasons to quicken his steps to be near his soulmate, his Kamayani whom he lovingly called Shraddha[29]. Today his mentors the great Saptrishis had sent a message urging him to step into his marital life.

His initial work was thought to be over and the Sages wanted him to enter personal bliss now. Manu too had

---

[28] Book ref. 'From Zero To One – The Story Of Manu' by MVG (Maneesha Agrawal)

[29] Literal meaning the one who's lord is Shradhhdev (Manu) Book ref. 'From Zero To One – The Story Of Manu' by MVG (Maneesha Agrawal)

realized that it was time for him to be attentive to his own household - his people were settled, his subjects were happy, and his Manali was prospering. Time had come for him to pay heed to another promise he had made to a reticent girl at the Boat Cliff years ago. He could be the husband to his wife now….Manu could think of Kamayani now.

"You have been standing at the door step since long it seems. I can't see why you do so every time I am expected to be back home. You have been here since mid-noon, right Shraddha?" Manu knew his wife and the passion she held for him.

"No. Eh...I just came around a few minutes earlier." She replied.

"Lying, as always." He nodded and smiled as he entered.

"N…no I am not lying. Not today Aaryaputra[30]." She contained her anxiety and followed her husband into the house.

She quickly walked to fetch something from inside and reappeared holding a silk-note (note written on a silk cloth) Aarya Prithu[31] (a chieftain) had asked her to give to Manu. It had some demarcations related to building construction science that were to be discussed and finalized in the meeting next morning.

[30] The Sanskrit term used by women to address their husbands (Aarya was for any male, but Aaryaputra = Aarya + Putra = son of an Aarya, was only for the husband)

[31] A respectable address for a male in general (not pertaining to a specific tribe)

Manu was seated on the bedstead. He looked affectionately at his lovely wife. She was wearing a white saree (a kind of wrap) with red and golden borders (she had decided to wear whites until they could consummate their marriage) and modest ornaments of gold in her wrists and neck. Creamy white pearls shone delicately within their gold braces she wore in her ears. Her long black tresses were tied in a loose Kapard (*a bun, coiffure*) that sat prettily on her neck. Her forehead flaunted a crimson dot that had always been the Manav King's focus for eyes whenever he could afford to…

How many times he had looked at that fiery stimulus which had inspired him like a sun brightening his horizon. How many times he had been tied to that small cusp…. the dot which ruled over him, as if tying him - restricting his world to its own petite realm. Manu was bemused at the effect of that little speck, and his unblinking eyes held their focus for long today…. making Kamayani wilt under the gaze.

"Here, you have a message from Aarya Prithu. Do …take a look Aaryaputra, for he wants to discuss and finalize it by tomorrow noon. Meanwhile I shall get you some fruits before dining. I can see the Sandhyavandan[32] time is approaching fast," she said nervously.

"No, no… I want nothing for now. Kamayani…."

"Hmm…?"

[32] A ritual of offering evening prayers (offered to the creator and thanking the sun for providing us the energy)

Manu was still caught in the small scarlet splendour on the flawless forehead. His senses fixed at it, he rose and reached for her hand. Lowering her eyes Kamayani shrunk a little. Manu stepped up slowly and drew her close. She gently pressed her head against his chest holding on tightly to the silk roll, and closed her eyes. Suddenly she trembled.... This was something new! She could hear his heart beat faster, louder for the first time in her life.... Manu was anxious!!

Sensing the jeopardy, Kamayani opened her eyes to realize Manu's palms holding her face. Lifting it to his own, he delicately planted a kiss on the forehead. ....the silk roll fell from her loosened fingers and she heard herself say as she stirred back,

"Don't, Aaryaputra! I ....It's difficult,"

"Kamayani....don't go Kaamayani. I....we..." he breathed and took a step forward. His fingers ran through her hair to let them loose grip of the Kapard and stray free,

"....Aaryaputra!"

"Listen to me, Kamayani. Sit here. Listen to the message I received from the Saptrishis today." his arms around his pulsating wife, Manu made her sit. Then kneeling by her side he gave her the reason to have allowed his heart to beat for a first time in his life.

The elegant Manav King wanted to see her as Shraddha today. He wanted to adorn her with flowers, accentuating the ethereal essence of her buoyant personality. He wanted to see her as the divine dream-girl - the one who had been sauntering sublimely over his sanities ever since he saw her for the first time at the banks of a raucous Arjikiya[33]. Today Manu wanted Shraddha to be illusory again. And suddenly he thought of something....

"Give me a while Kamayani....I have some work that needs attention. I will be back soon enough. I promise - before the Sandhyavandan," said Manu and rushed out of his abode much to the bewilderment of his wife.

[33] Book reference 'From Zero To One – The Story Of Manu' by MVG (Maneesha Agrawal)

CHAPTER 6

COLLISION OF PATHS

I

Manu was heading to the other banks of Arjikiya where he knew plenty of Kairavs[34] blossomed during the season. He wanted to pick a handful to embellish his fantasy ... a longing which was prepared to emerge out of its self-imposed slumber. He wanted to drape his wife with the magnificence of white, signifying the purest form of lovely emotions their hearts held for each other.

He plunged into the river waters and crossed over to the other side of the stream, where a snowy camouflage bloomed beseeching the Manav King's interest. Hundreds of majestic Kairavs stood bowing to him, inviting his eyes to judge their utility for him.

Manu picked his handful and did his Sandhyavandan there as the sun was slipping fast to retreat. Holding the flowers carefully he swam back faster, eager to return to his village.

The stately Manav King was hurrying his way when he collided with a human form abruptly. One Kairav from the bunch slipped out of his clutch. Adjusting the remaining flowers carefully and backing a few steps to

---

[34] White lotus

identify the stranger, he looked at a very foreign face peering at him!

II

Ira was strolling alongside the river banks when she thought she heard someone make a splash into the waters. As she made her search for the source she suddenly collided with someone before she could know.

She stepped back and saw the imperial figure of a man....dressed in a white Dhoti (wrap) with a golden waistband. His wet white stole hung glued to his marvellously set square shoulders, and his long arms held a flower bunch delicately. His dark mane flocked his slickly chiselled face, and his glistening forehead bore a sun-sign crayoned with a bright yellow.

His piercing eyes looked dramatically from under his wet eyelashes, and his intense voice rung some chord inside her when he said, "Pardon my inaccuracy Shubhe[35], I just overstepped!"

Ira stared speechless.

"I....did I hurt you?" Manu was apologetic.

"...."

"Namaskar Shubhe. You do not seem to belong here. Where are you coming from?"

Mechanically Ira picked up the fallen flower from the ground and held it in front of her eyes,

---

[35] Address for any young lady in Vedic times

"Can it be mine?" she uttered.

"What? .....Oh yes, why not. Of course you can keep this one for yourself, and I can arrange for many more if you would want. We are Manavas and this is our region called Manali. You seem to be coming from a foreign land. Allow me to extend our hospitality to you… we shall be delighted to have you as our guests at Manali. I am Manu, the leader of this habitat."

"….Manu? And I am Ira. I've come here looking for..." She answered dreamily.

"Yes..?"

Ira wanted to say 'you', which was lost in her throat. All her senses had given up to her eyes. She couldn't think, say or hear anything….she could only see Manu.

Nadia, who was looking for the Princess spotted Ira's interaction with a stranger from at a distance. She came hurried along,

"Greetings Aarya. I am Nadia, companion to Princess Ira of the Causeruman region. She is the daughter of Great Asur King Shambarasur. We are travelling around foreign lands to see more of this world. This is the first time during all these six months that our Caravan came across a human habitat. Thank you Aarya for your invite, as our Princess herself is eager to see a culture and civilization different from ours. Ira, isn't that so? ....Ira?" Nadia shook Ira's arm who was still in a trance.

"Ye…yes that is so…yes of course!" Ira attended.

"Swagat[36] Atithi[37]!" Manu folded his hands and formally invited his guests after getting the introduction, "I shall arrange a reception for you and the Caravan as soon as I get back to my village. Please be our guests till the time you wish to stay at the Himalayas. We shall be gratified by your presence at Manali", said he and left for making requisite arrangements.

Nadia gazed at her friend's face as she stood watching Manu depart. She saw something in her face that induced an idea in to the wiser girl's head. Ira had looked absolutely entranced.

"…Ira?"

"Hmm?"

"Ira, I do not think it is wise."

"What is not wise? ....our going to their village Manali? You think we should've invited them here instead?"

"Really!"

"Yes?"

"Ira….I don't think it is wise to fall for a stranger that easily. Now be angry at my surmise if you like!" Nadia never minced words.

---

[36] Meaning welcome in Sanskrit
[37] Guests in Sanskrit

"What on earth do you...." She glared at her with smouldering eyes but suddenly big tears rolling down her cheeks surprised herself, "I... eh...what on earth..."

"Let's get back to the pavilion before everyone is here." Nadia held her hand and made her turn towards her marquee.

III

Ira and Nadia sat beside each other in their pavilion erected on the lower banks of Arjikiya. The sudden and somewhat rude inferring of Ira's feelings by Nadia had hurt them both.

Ira felt wedged, and Nadia felt guilty of wedging through her friend's tender heart. The two had cried for a while and now sat comforting each other.

"Ira! I am very, very sorry for being unnecessarily curt. I know I was ....I was very, awfully rude to you. Forgive me my gentle princess, please forgive me if you can. I can't say why I did this to you... maybe I got a bit too worried for you and I....I just overdid. I am so sorry, my gentle Ira. Please look at me.....here... Forgive your silly Nadia will you?" she sobbed holding her friend's hand. Her broad, flat face looked surprisingly unfamiliar whenever she was emotional.

"Na... Nadia. I'm fine. Oh yes....I am okay. I know you mean good to me. You've always been good."

"Thank you Ira. I....I shall never be so impulsive again - promise."

"Yes. And you must try to trust me more… I shall have nothing that I'll hide from you. This is my promise to you."

"O my Ira! This is why I love you the most under this expansive sky." Nadia kissed her Princess's hands.

They were reassuring each other when Damas knocked and entered the cabin saying that a bunch of some people called Manavas, led by a certain 'Som' has arrived to take them to a certain village Manali.

IV

Manu had hurried back to his village and arranged for a few people led by Som (his closest aide) to bring the visitors to Manali. He gave the charge to Aaryá[38] Dhriti (Prithu's wife) to organize the dwellings and other comforts for the guests. Having done with the responsibilities, Manu returned to his cliff and found Kamayani as always, standing at the doorstep.

"I knew you will be here. It took me longer than expected and yet I find you standing at the doorstep tiring yourself as always," he complained.

"No Aaryaputra I am not tired at all."

"Won't you ask me what took me so long?"

"Only if you would want to tell me". She smiled.

And then he told her about the day's chance meeting with the Princess of Causeruman Ira, daughter of Shambarasur.

[38] For addressing ladies, Aaryaa – with an extra 'a'

"Shambarasur…," Kamayani tried to remember, "the one who has the infamous stone castle built upon the ruins of an erstwhile peaceful Causeruan civilization?"

"You have heard about him?"

"Yes I know something of his background. He was a notorious name in the Asur dynasty during the early days of Aditya/Asur conflicts. He fought against Taat[39] Shakra (Aditya leader) in that fierce combat with the Asur king Madasur[40] near the coast of Saurashtra[41] (where river Saraswati emptied into the western sea). The Asuras lost the battle, and Madasur was killed by Taat Shakra. But his chief commander Shambarasur had survived and is believed to have fled to some far off unknown place. He had captured some foreign region unjustly so I heard. I know this much, but am not aware of the whereabouts of the region or any details further."

"Hmm…looks like this Causeruman is the region he invaded."

"This visitor… Ira… She is his daughter?"

"Yes, her companion says so. What would you suggest Kamayani? How should we treat them?"

"Why…naturally like any other guest. There's no reason to associate an old story from a bygone era to a present day liaison."

---

[39] Address for a fatherly figure
[40] Shakra's famous enemy
[41] Modern day Gujrat

"My Shraddha....! Only you can be so clear in your thoughts. I also coincide with what you say," he pecked her forehead once and assigning her duties for the evening's guest-welcome assembly went out of the chalet with quick steps.

CHAPTER 7
GUESTS AT MANALI

I

Ira's Caravan received a grand welcome at Manali.

They were greeted with cheerful flower decorations at this first Manav village. Interesting rituals of salutation were carried out as the whole village got assembled at the village hall (central place) to receive the guests. The guests were garlanded with fresh flowers and red sandal-wood paste was applied to the men folk's foreheads (a gesture of offering regard). Incense sticks were lit imparting a perfumed extravagance to the already appeasing atmosphere.

The festive air at Manali held a classy opulence, far from the artless Asur civilities Ira was sick of viewing. The Manav people came elegantly decked up in colourful fineries, embroidered wraps and tasteful stoles. Their women and children sported attractive hair stylings and men wore bright headgears.

They all looked so beautiful, smiling and adorable.

All Manavas, particularly Kamayani were devoted to the comforts of visitors. They offered the bemused travellers luscious servings of Yava-Apoop (a kind of pancake made of honey, milk and millet cereal) Odanam (a milk and rice dish), and other delectable vegetable preparations for dinner. The ingredients though unheard of and unexperienced by the visitors, were thoroughly enjoyed by them.

After the ceremonious dinner, an entertaining grandeur of singing and dancing followed.

Highlighting the day's celebrations to honour the arrival of Ira's Caravan into their region, the Manavas sang melodious songs and danced gracefully to the sonorous notes of Mridang (drum), flute, and Mohanveena (a string instrument) playing in harmony. Kamayani sat close to Ira and Nadia, and explained the significance of various rituals and songs that were being presented to welcome them. She continuously upheld her visitor's interest in each aspect of Manav culture that they were being presented with.

For Ira and Nadia the symbolic meaning of every song, every dance and even the dress-up was equally mesmerising as were the presentations. Everything was so fantastic, elegant, grand and out of the world. Certainly - this was a different world they had come into.

Ira was overjoyed and highly impressed. She was thrilled to the core but… Ah! For her restless eyes… they could manage only a fleeting glimpse of Manu who was seated beyond Kamayani.

Tonight he was himself a spectacle. His already captivating pull was augmented by his prolific head-dress of red brocade which he wore with a striking gold and pearl accessory pinned to its left. A sturdy (braced) sword dangled by his side, tied to his golden waistband.

He looked amazingly regal, stately, riveting. Ira was absolutely engaged....taken in by his charms, his people and his land.

II

The two foreign girls were resting in their comfortable room after the revelries were over and the night had intensified.

They were both happy. After so many months, they were able to find a civilization so different from theirs. And they had liked it too. What a drastic change it was between the two populace - the Manavas on one hand were a disciplined urbane society and Asuras on the other hand were diametrically opposite - riotous and rustic!

The people at Manali were a set of self-abstemious people who realized the value of living. They were regarding life as something precious and devout, an outlook which had reflected through their ceremonious merriments. Quite visibly for them life wasn't as frivolous to be thrown away in a punching rink! Where was the need for that boisterous cruelty Asuras believed essential for survival? How was the Asura's nasty callousness a requirement for enjoying the pleasures of life.... a bequest which the astute Manavas seemed to have been celebrating so humbly? What did the Asuras take their lives as – a projectile canister waiting to be destroyed by a head-on collision some day? Preposterous!

The Manavas at Manali were a civil society – whilst the Asuras were the uncultured lot. They knew naught apart from spending their whole lives thinking of nothing! For them life meant nothing beyond fulfilling their famishments of hunger, lust and power. The Asuras were severely primitive in their thoughts and beliefs… and absolutely lame in their methods and conduct. For once today, Ira and Nadia both were thinking alike.

"It is so different and gay here Nadia. These people look so controlled and so happy! They have none of that pompous arrogance…..the barbaric viciousness which I hate to see in our Asuras. They look so sombre and appear to be living as a civilized society – something that I've always wanted to be a part of. I'd say they are pretty disciplined and dutiful as though don't even need a King to rule them. I would apply the same principle to our lot – but in an opposite sense. You know, I often think why do we ever need a King….I mean we are still unscrupulous, disorderly, lawless and so wayward?"

"Yes, I can see the point. And maybe that is what we Asuras are – the intractable headstrong tribe who like to survive being difficult."

"Bah! Being difficult… that's what they are! I remember the nanny – and I've always thought she looked more like you," said Ira with a twinkle in her eyes, "she told me virtues and traits of people one cannot imagine at our Causeruman. I…..I am sure she was talking about the Manavas. Even my mother had belonged to a similar culture, she had said. My mother was an Aarya[42] girl....? Nadia, could this be the identity I was craving for all through my life?"

"Oh.... I shouldn't say that, but you have something there. This is a very curious place we've come to. And surely I cannot but like the way they live. I also faintly remember some of the stories even my grandma used to tell me about the people of Aryavart when I was very young. She told me that our ancestors had branched out from these very people many years ago."

"Hmm...yes, the peaceful people of a peaceful region. Captivating though they are!" Ira was suddenly quite - quieter than expected.

"Ira...?" abruptly Nadia tugged at her.

"...Umm?"

"Look here, let us go back in a day or two."

"Go back? No. Why? I mean we still have at least a month before we must start our journey back."

"Yes.... we do have time. But I wonder what time may have for us if we continue being here?"

"Now what does that mean?"

"Ira, my dear! I know it is so lively and lovely here. I know how you feel....even I am feeling the alluring warmth of this strange place. But I am scared. For it's much too good and nice here. We...we may not belong you see. It is always wise not to get excessively

---

[42] Natives of Aaryavart

engrossed in a sphere where one does not belong. Ira, after all one day we have to be back… to live with our own people. We must be back. So I think before we start getting further prejudiced ….."

"….Prejudiced? Why should we be prejudiced? Really, the things you can think of!" She got up and searching for something here-n-there ruined the seriousness of the conversation, "…and where did you keep my Lo…Kairav…Lotus that day?" Ira wasn't even listening to Nadia now!

"Lotus? What Lotus?"

"The one that the Manav King gave me? I told you to put it in a water bath….and I simply can't find it here!"

"Eh…!" Nadia glared disbelievingly at the Princess's childishly worried face and nodded several times before she stood up searching for the said flower. She could sense for sure, they were heading for some big trouble at Manali.

III

Manu had to leave Manali for a few days immediately the next morning. There was a sudden confusion over the water channelization management at an ongoing construction site.

A river-canal system was being devised for ensuring perineal water supply to their farther farmlands. Water from the nearby source which was the river, was getting conducted in channels to these newly laid farmlands serving for irrigational purposes during dry season. But it was found that the water carried heaps of silt along with its flow. To counter this they had to think of desilting methods. Hence Manu and Prithu were called at the site for guidance and detailed discussions.

At getting a message our proficient Manav Leader left straightaway with Prithu and few of his aides in the early hours of dawn.

This time Manu was going to be missed by Kamayani, and equally by the Causeruman Princess Ira (who secretly in her heart had decided to wait for him till his return at Manali). She 'couldn't leave without seeing him once more', she had thought. Her people including the obedient Damas were issued to return and wait at their base-camp while Ira and Nadia continued staying at the village.

Ira had staunchly expressed her desire to see this remarkable world of Manavas more closely (or so she had argued at least), and Nadia easily consented in the wake of Manu's absence....whose proximity she had feared for some very definite reason. 'It will drive that silly infatuation out of her head. Of course I know what she's got there for him. At least by staying close to the Manav King's lovely wife Kamayani she will realize her position', Nadia had actually been happy.

Next few days the two girls spent observing the Manav community closely.

The Asur girls devoted long hours watching the Manavas perfect their art of living. They had never come across such a beautifully synchronized social system of living. Ira saw them work hard in their vast fields and observed them nurse their cattle. She noticed that they appeared to be talking to their cattle herd as if they were 'some part of their extended family! While our Asuras treat fellow beings as if they were mere cattle?' It amused her.

Rising early (excitingly new for her) Ira learned to pray at the Arjikiya with the early risers of Manali, and enjoyed thanking the surreal sun supremely plunging into the credulous river-waters in the evenings. She relished the fruits, cereals and other simply cooked fare which this incredible community of non-violent people dished up every day for their rare, infrequent guests. She loved the simple yet decorous sarees the Manav women wore and even tried to change her own guise once! She tried tying a saree, rolled her hair into a loose bun in an attempt to look like one of them, wanting to be one of them. Who knows, her heart might be nurturing a dream to remain there....for a long and a longer time.

Nadia, supporting her Princess's amusements was relieved. Watching her rejoice even in the absence of Manu in her new found environs Nadia was able to dismiss Ira's clearly evident excitement as a child's delight. She thought of her superfluous tendencies as a part of that juvenile human curiosity which gets attracted to simple changes in dressing and dinning routines. But this girl was perhaps unaware of the strange and exceedingly clever workings of heart which were certainly at play here!

Kamayani and other women folk were aiding the new-comers within their everyday quests. They were very forthcoming in helping them understand the ecosphere and the tenets behind their whole subsistence. They helped the visitors grasp the quintessence of Manav culture which was centred at celebrating the real spirit of worthy living. The Asur girls were seeing the difference – the amoral anarchy of Causeruman v/s sanctified scruples of Manav society.

It was over a week now and despite all her new-found pleasures Ira wasn't happy.

An anonymous restlessness was gaining momentum somewhere inside. She was expecting something …. Probably which was coming to her, but was not clear. A discomforting edginess was playing upon her calm, as if her heart was at loggerheads with her peace. She wanted company but not Nadia's – she wanted to stay forever at Manali but not without…. Manu?

She was speculating this absurd commotion within herself, when one evening Nadia decided to persuade Ira to leave the village finally.

"Ira, I think we have seen much of the world now. And we've seen a very nice happy little community of adorable Manavas too. Now what about returning to our own land? You must remember the promise you made to your Father….we should start preparing for our journey backway."

"Backway? It is so early to talk about it right now. Why, it's just been a couple of days….I'm sure we can afford spending some more time here. Oh Nadia….! Must we always remember it? Can't you ever think of something else?" said the Princess dramatically encircling Nadia's neck with her delicate fair arms.

Nadia looked at Ira's comely smiling face and twinkling blue eyes fluttering persuasively at her. Disarmed, she gently removed her hold and kissed the Princess's hands,

"Right okay. We will not talk about going back to Causeruman presently."

"Great. You know, this is the only opportunity for us to see one of the Creator's better creations. Nadia, just look at the place we've landed in to….the softer hues of red green and gold on the land… and brilliance of a completely unpretentious sun securing the cool blue of the sky… No rambling races, no howling fights. The air is sweetly scented, and carries a bloom so serene. It…it feels as if we were in some celestial heaven! Add to it such wonderfully interesting people gelling in so well with Nature here – always smiling and contended with life!"

"You make it sound so magical….and yet you are right. I too admit that this is going to be the most fascinating experience I'm likely to have in my entire life."

"Aha! And there's more to it I feel. There is so much to know about them, so much to learn from them… one can just not get enough of anything here!"

"Yes. That is true. But do you realize my dear Ira, we have been staying here for so long. It might be slightly inconvenient to our hosts even if they don't let us know," She was trying to cajole Ira into returning (before Manu came back for an underlying fear of hers), "If you agree, we can go back to our own campsite at the lower banks of the river and still continue staying close to them – that will be the outskirts of Manali."

"Nay….I can't go. I won't." she said with her child like candour.

"You can't? Or you won't?" Nadia scrutinized her face. Her beady eyes were suddenly alert, searching keenly.

"Oh goodness Nadia! Only I don't see why you have to be so….so…" her irritation was held by the sudden arrival of a message from Kamayani saying that the Manav King was back today and the guests were invited to join the evening feast at the village Hall (it was their custom to celebrate their King's return by having supper together with him at the central place).

IV

Manu exchanged pleasantries with the guests warmly, without being aware of his magnetic pull on one of them. He conversed with them affably with his usual refined manner and attended to their wellbeing at his village.

The dinner was over. The assembly dispersed after a detailed discussion was held on matters the group had gone out to sort. Separate tanks for desilting were to be dug and maintained for depositing the river water before it would enter the fields – they had concluded.

Ira and Nadia had opted to stay during the discussions as they were also curious on studying the way the Manavas were engineering water supply systems scientifically. Ira of course, had more of a personal reason.

Finally Manu got up and walked away with Kamayani to his abode at the boat cliff, her hand held in his. The principal couple of Manavas was absolutely majestic in their stride….they looked perfect together, and made for each other. They seemed entirely in love though refrained from any public proximity or reckless display of informal emotions.

Manu was home to Shraddha after a long gap and today he wanted to make it up for his prolonged absence. He stopped her on reaching their doorstep,

"Umm…not so early Shraddha. I do not want to get in. It is so pleasant here outside. See that glorious moon brightening up our sky….I want to get drenched in this magnificent moonlight tonight. With you. Will you?"

Kamayani answered looking into his eyes that smiled quietly. The two sat beneath the gaily lit sky sprinkling streams of silvery moonlight over the verve of life on the Earth. This was certainly a heaven….a heaven of love, faith and respect for life and respect for the ones living under the munificence of the whole expanse.

V

What could be said of Ira tonight, who was completely disoriented. She was far away from herself, her Nadia, her attentions and her reflexions!

Everything whirled around her senses …she could make nothing of her strange yearning for the proximity of that one person – Manav King Manu. She had seen him tonight after a gap of few days…and realized how she had longed! His charm seemed to have multiplied many folds since the last time she had seen him. His red head dress pulled her, and the pearl and gold accessory pinned her! The handsome Manav King was stupendous, magnetic, and overpowering tonight.

No matter how hard she tried but Ira had not been able to take her eyes off him.

The gathered crowd seemed inconspicuous…. Kamayani and Nadia didn't matter, her own conduct as the Causeruman Princess was immaterial. Her eyes had held their centre unabashedly and unblinkingly today.

And Manu…? He had barely looked at her. This had tweaked her aching the worse way. What on earth was the matter with her….what was happening to her?

Sitting at her guest-lodging in Manali that night and struggling with self, she found herself irritated beyond reason when Nadia tried to make her speak -

"If you would come out of your meditation and let me know the cause of distress, I promise I can help you."

"You think you can think of everything....don't you?" Ira snapped.

Nadia, the very wise companion to the royal girl wasn't rattled – she had actually anticipated the outburst. She replied softly "No. I do not think of anything that you do not want me to."

Placated by the undertone Ira responded "I....I didn't mean to be rude. I just thought I can take a walk around the cliffs if you wouldn't mind..." turning her face and before Nadia could speak she had hurried out of the room.

Ira strolled around the higher cliffs of Manali lost in her own thoughts. Her heart was stinging and her mind blank. There was a disturbing heaviness of unreserved emotions.... churning hard within.

She was struggling, trying to curb her frenzied anxieties when a little ahead of her she saw a neat abode perched on a raised cliff. It was home to a couple who revelled in each other's company, oblivious to the sufferings of desperate hearts. They glorified devotion, together immersed in the white light of a beautiful full moon on that scintillating night at Manali. Ira saw Manu holding Kamayani in his long arms....her chin was held in his fingers and their lips were engaged. Ira stood at a distance. And stayed fixed....jaded, jammed.

CHAPTER 8
IRA

I

Ever since the return of Ira and Nadia to their basecamp pavilion at the banks of Arjikiya everything had changed. Ira was very quiet.

It were three days now that she was dallying as if in a shock. Nadia had guessed the reason, but she couldn't risk another face-off by being blunt this time. She was a clever companion easily could assign the reason to what her small watchful eyes had been noticing. They had seen the draw Manav King was wielding on her Princess ever since their first interaction.

Till now Nadia was waiting before she could touch the right note at the right time. She had delayed attention to the topic purposefully, to allow it to let go of....pass away on its own. Had she pressed persistently, Ira was sure to pursue it even more staunchly knowing her stubborn-ness.

But now it was high time – Ira was clearly reeling under deep stress caused by her fixations, which could be love or infatuation or that naive attraction of having met someone very ....very different. 'Matters could be better handled only when they get clearer', Nadia was thinking.

Now that it was time to know what exactly the matter was she decided upon the need to make Ira talk, "You may have to finally abandon that white Lotus…your Kairav or whatever it is called here. See, it is useless now …turning stale and numb." Nadia started.

"Kairav? ….o yes. No…I mean, no. We cannot throw it away. I rather love this one."

"I can ask Damas to bring you some fresh flowers from the other side of the river if you want. There are plenty of these growing that side."

"But I just want this one."

"Oh Ira! It is not good…not at all good for you. You know this, don't you?"

Ira lifted her eyes to meet her friend's…. Nadia saw the sapphire blue glistened with emotions. Her cherubic face was stressed under a burden, and her lips trembled with apprehension. As if she was in two minds… to speak or not to.

Nadia slowly sat by Ira's side and comforted her round face in her steady palms, "Do not look so laden, Ira. I am here to take care of you. Tell me all dear ….today tell me everything about it. I can assure you that even as I know what you are going through, I want you to tell me all that you're having inside. Take it out. It… it is hurting you real bad… I know it is probably more than you can handle."

"…"

"Listen here Ira. Look at me. I know what it is with you. I know… I know why this Kairav means so much to you and why you sit holding it for the whole day. Tell me all you can my dear Princess. You know I will help ….oh you must. Please my precious Ira, trust me here today. Won't you?"

Princess Ira of Causeruman erupted into sobs. She slid her face in the comforting arms of Nadia and snivelled her burdens on the shoulders of her long trusted companion. She cried her heart out without a word of protest as she let the other girl take charge of her. For, it was clear that Nadia had known everything much earlier all along.

The two friends sat composedly in each other's refuge after a while. Ira got steadier when she had unburdened herself and her eyes had emptied out all the streams of kept-unkempt emotions they were flooded with.

"Nadia," said the Princess, "I am becoming a stranger to my own self… someone you may not even know… you …you saw nothing! I… if I tell you… If I do I won't have a face to show you…"

"Nay….you need never say so dear one." Nadia was gently wiping away redundant tears from her cheeks.

"It is going to be so when I tell you why. I wanted… wanted to... Oh Lord! I cannot."

"You will tell me nothing that I do not know. Trust me my dear, I know. And I know you more than even yourself. So tell me now…"

"Nadia I wanted his arms around me that night when I saw him so close to Kamayani!" Ira cried out closing her eyes tight.

Unbroken strings of tears ran incessantly down her face, "Can you believe Nadia how I felt? I felt....it ...it should be me not her. Into that place... those long arms around me... my chin in his fingers... and his lips touching mine!" her voice died.

Nadia was shocked at the flagrancy of the desire coiled up in her friend's heart. Whatever extent she had thought Ira's infatuation for the Manav King went up to... was certainly not this. Manu's charm had pierced beyond the periphery of Ira's heart... The fascination had turned into a fervent craving. It was bound to burn her core if left unattended.

Not realizing so a few days earlier Nadia may have advised her to leave the place immediately and forget all about Manali Manava and Manu. But now that the layers of her heart were emerging visible she could see how serious the lesion was! Nadia had to act, do something. Thinking for a few minutes she asked Ira,

"Is it so serious Ira?"

"I do not know what you ask....but I can tell you that I can't think of anything else."

"Hmm."

"I feel it...Nadia, oh I know. I will not live without him. I cannot. Maybe I've come here destined to be doomed... for I can't leave this place and I do not know the next…! I can see how hopeless it sounds, but there it is."

"Ira…"

"I …I realized that day Nadia what I wanted out of this strange pull, this odd captivation I was jaded with every time I saw Aarya Manu."

"Would you want to marry him?"

"Marry…? Whom?"

"Of course Aarya Manu! You can marry him."

"Me… real… you…?"

"Yes why not? You my dear Ira, are free to marry any person of your choice in or out of the community as the rest of Asur girls are. And you do not need anyone's permission to do so as per our customs. It isn't complicated…all one has to do is a mutual exchange of garlands… And then you are married! So tell me, would you want to get married to Manu?" Nadia was thinking very fast.

"But… but he is already married?"

"So what, men are known to marry twice or even thrice …provided you are open to the idea of attuning it with Kamayani."

"Y…yes of course. But I… can I…." she stammered.

Ira was struck numb with the possibility of getting married to the man of her dreams. The thought took time to seep-in to her conscious and when it did, her girlish spirit was revived. She was ecstatic – muted with the fanciful effect.

But next followed a counter thought that of her father, Manu or maybe Kamayani not accepting the proposition. She was again ridden with timorous emotions - joyful, shocking, disbelief, credulous – almost child-like,

"Really Nadia! Can I? Really?"

"Eh…why not? Yes, if you want."

"And father? What about him? What is he going to say?"

"Nothing. You have known many Asur Princesses who married on their own… you will be doing nothing out of ordinary. Our great King Shambarasur is absolutely easy-going and I'm sure he will understand."

"And Kamayani? And Manu? Will they consent? Does he like me?" this thought then impeded the cheery ecstasy that was beginning to rise in Ira's heart. It unnerved her once again and made her slide back to her overwrought anxiety.

Although Nadia was quick to counter with a "who wouldn't like you once he has seen you", something plunged down in the depth of Ira's heart.

II

Next day Manu received a message from the Causeruman camp. Damas had carried an invite for the Manav King to come to their pavilion for some deliberations of a personal kind, so that he need not have his subjects along with. This was not so unusual as the Manavas were a growing and forthcoming community. They had shown openness for any kind of cultural and/or traditional exchange with other communities which might be the case, Manu and Kamayani had thought.

So on that very fine spring evening our eminent Manav King went alone to the visitor camp at the lower banks of Arjikiya.

III

Manu came back almost too immediately. His naturally composed stride was overdone… apparently fraught with some weight under his composure. Something was there that had bothered him.

The Manav King was not able to believe what had been proposed to him a few moments ago at the Causeruman camp. He repetitively shook his head as if trying to deny the day's overture – and walked with a peculiar stiffness. Finally as if rejecting the lingering discomfort with a wave of his hand, he entered his cottage followed by Kamayani who stood (at the doorstep, as usual) watching him curiously.

Manu got seated with downcast eyes. He, as if arranging his thoughts took a while to look at his wife. Then choosing his words he said slowly -

"Nothing was actually the matter. It was something of an altogether different nature err… peculiar rather." said he with a hesitation atypical of him.

"Oh…yes?"

"Kamayani, I… I can't think what to say, or whether to say."

"Tell me only if you want to, Aaryaputra." she rose and prepared to move to fetch him some food and water, as the evening was about to advance into night.

Manu stood to stop Kamayani. He stepped up closer and paused. As if waiting with closed eyes before deciding carefully on his words he said, "The Causeruman Princess wants to marry me. Her companion said so. This is the reason they had called me today. She says that girl…. Ira, she loves me?"

The wife cleared her knitted brows. She laughed and looked even more adorably into her husband's shy eyes saying, "And why not! Nothing wrong with it… who wouldn't love my lord…! The best among mortals! So would she, or any other girl," she chuckled mischievously enjoying Manu's discomfort thoroughly!

Manu was struggling to face her now and the reticent Manav King's gaze dropped to the ground.

"…so what did you answer her with?" Kamayani was loving his timidity, "Aryaputra! If you've come to ask for my permission for a YES, I am ready to accept her in our household. Though with a few conditions which I…."

Manu's hand clasped her mouth before she could say further, "must you go on torturing me for something that I haven't done?"

He slid his arm around her and kissed her magnificent eyes close murmuring, "Shradhhdev Manu shall only love Shraddha till the day there is life under the sun."

CHAPTER 9
DESPERATION

I

It broke Nadia's heart to see her. Ira was not the same high bred Princess Ira of Causeruman – she was a forlorn, weary wanderer who seemed to have lost her way. Her eyes lacked their lustre and her face lost its colour. Her golden locks fought alone with the confines of loneliness she had submitted herself to, as she would utter nothing for long hours. And whenever she did it was in monosyllables. She would walk out of her camp restricting everyone (including Nadia) from following her, and trek. Where? To nowhere.

Nadia was having a hard time trying to follow Ira without her knowledge which she did invariably. She saw Ira walk on random cliffs, her tears fighting her yearning. Nadia would then reach her, hold her hands and try to comfort her with a muted tenderness that was so unlike Nadia.

Quite irrationally Ira had refused to move from the place at all. The Caravan was staying put for no reason plausible to any member of the crew. As the time to begin their return journey was approaching near Nadia saw how futile and stupid it was to keep staying there. It was like lurking with a hope which can never meet completion. But then matters of heart have been known to take a toll on every reason, each logic, every sense. She could do nothing.

It was a delightful evening. The jaunty wind currents happily drew the scent of magnificent lotus bloom to every trajectory of the beautiful landscape. Sparks of life rejoiced, and the picturesque panorama around Arjikiya was dyed in soft golden effects of slowly subsiding sunlight.

Ira walked without being aware of where she was heading to. Her eyes were arid and dry, for they had been tussling hard with their emotions.

Where will her fixation lead her to? ...Where was her passion pulling her? What hope had in store for her....? What was desolation bringing to her?

She did not want any answers. She was stuck and stranded, caught in the captivation of her own caprices. Her inward upheaval was restricting her from being attentive to the calls of the outside world...

"Ooo... watch it! Stop! I say hold your step.... Stop!" someone was calling trying to pull her from her thoughts. She stopped with a jerk, and turned to see the Manav King Manu rushing at her.

"Where could you have landed Shubhe! You are on the edge!" He had shouted.

"I am on the edge... yes, maybe. I am on the edge!" on an impulse she turned her head back to see the path her feet followed. It had ended. A deep – horrifyingly deep gorge lay beneath her feet! She was standing on the edge of a fatally dangerous cleft.

"You... are you okay? Here... hold my hand. You need help..." Manu was extending his arm at her.

Ira blinked to see what was real....? Was the edge real, or Manu's hand extended to her was real? Her vision seem to be seized.

But she took too long to decide... and her rescuer saw the need to act fast. He pulled the annexed girl out of her reserve and hauled her to safety with a "Come along, there... there... you are safe," she had heard him say.

Ira swayed with disbelief... and fell to the ground. She lifted her golden head and shivered under the shadow of Manu's figure that was sheltering her at the moment. It must be a dream!

But there he was, standing tall covering her form right in front of her. His black hair-locks flew freely around his attractive handsome face. He was more than majestic standing in front of her facing the east so that the west-bound reddened sun bore him his red headdress...!

Ira couldn't handle the multiplied effect. She froze kneeling by his side and stared disbelievingly...

"You are all right Shubhe? Shall I... or wait. I'll fetch you some water. It's nothing but the shock," he said and turned to move.

Ira remembered… she had clung on to his hand mumbling, "Don't go".

Manu stopped. He looked at the foreign girl beckoning his attention. He saw for the first time, here were very dark blue eyes… gone azure with emotion.

"Shubhe", said he firmly, "the Princess of Causeruman deserves better attention than I can give her. Please rise. And do not make Manu the culprit of disregarding a lady."

"…" her throat choked with tears, "Aa… Aarya Manu, you can..."

"I can give you nothing Shubhe,"

"You… you can. Aarya Manu….you can. One thing… just give me… give me the right to love you. Aarya Manu… give me the right to live with you… for you. I… I want nothing…nothing Aarya Manu… I want only to see you… be here… close to you… it is only you Aarya Manu… only you… " she had went on to say everything she wanted to.

Manu stood motionless. He was nervous. The greatest Manav King felt scared while handling an emotional outburst arranged by certain complexities of heart. He himself could not imagine a way to withstand such a barren desperation… he wasn't equipped to handle it.

"Gather yourself Shubhe. I implore you." he could barely say.

"J…just one thing Aarya Manu. On…only that... I… I will love you… I really will... for the rest of my life… I will live till I can be in love with you…." said a broke voice, and a wet face pressed against his hand. "Oh I want nothing… nothing else from you… Aarya Manu…," Ira went on sobbing hysterically and clenching his hand tightly close to her mouth.

Manu stood unmoved. He had never felt so helpless.

Nadia reached the spot searching for her princess and found the two stuck – one with her emotional surge and the other with his dilemma!

The wise girl saw the edge and acted quickly… she released Manu's hand from Ira's grip and arrested her fall in safe arms.

"Sorry Aarya Manu," Nadia said, "I am so sorry on her behalf. She is in a difficult state now-a-days. Please take no notice of today's indelicacy. I…I must thank you for saving her life."

The Manav King walked away with a very heavy heart. He had unintentionally intruded upon a star-crossed visitor who had entered his realm by chance, and who very unfortunately got inflicted with pain, distress, dejection - an agonizing mayhem of overpowering emotions… all because of him. He was never so disturbed.

Manu was at the centre of all this turbulence but he was clueless on how he could help. He could do nothing – nothing at all to relieve Ira of the suffering she underwent. He knew how hard the girl was struggling… how intense her agony was and yet he couldn't help. He was in love with his wife. Nothing on earth was going to change it – now or never. Where was a scope for someone else's inclusion into their lives? What could be done for a person who wants to have the unavailable?

It was cruel the way emotions played their hand. How eccentric were the inducements of Nature sometimes and how bizarrely they worked?

II

Nadia was trying her best to dissuade Ira from sinking into further dejection, but this is exactly what was happening. Her wanton obsessions were posing threats to her life now.

Not that the Manav King was unworthy of the feelings Ira had for him but he had clearly said that he would never love Ira… nor marry her. He had pledged marrying once only, and nothing was going to change his resolve. The day when Nadia had proposed Ira's alliance to him he had said, 'I can only love once, and shall ever marry once – which I already am to the only girl I love.'

The fascination Ira had for Manu was killing her day by day. That evening Nadia realized how close Ira had come to losing her life. She was actually yes, living on the edge.

With no solution neither a respite in the offing Nadia decided to leap in… she must plan something more explicit, she had concluded. In the privacy of their pavilion that night she said to Ira,

"Do you realize... you could have died today?"

"I might as well."

"... Ira?"

"...."

"Is it that irreversible Ira? Can't you come out of it? Can you just not forget Manu and this wretched place Manali? Ira, he doesn't love you. We... we will go to our Causeruman. We have our people, your father, we will find love and be happy once again....me and you?"

"...."

"Listen Ira, try to believe me. I am telling you... we will be very happy once we go back to our own land."

"Nadia...Oh! My good Nadia! I ...I know it is no good thinking about Aarya Manu over and over again. But I can't! ...honest! I can't live without him. Believe me... I... I might forever be in love Nadia... hopelessly... endlessly."

Nadia stared in exasperation. She perceived the futility of explaining reasoning to a love-struck maiden!

"Oh... why don't you understand Nadia! I cannot go from here... away from Aarya Manu. He will not have me. But me, I have to be close to him. Forever ....to see him, to be in love with him. I... I just have to be here." Ira was saying rhetorically.

"Okay. I see how serious it is. Let me think of something then."

"Think of something? Like what…?"

"….like lifting him away from Manali and taking him to Causeruman!"

"WHAT?"

"Yes, why not? You are not allowed to join his household, so we will make him join ours!"

"Nadia… seriously! Are you … you're out of your senses? Why will Aarya Manu come with us to Causeruman? And moreover…. he is not a child of five whom you can lift! How do you think…Lord! Why…what is wrong with you?"

"Nothing is wrong with me. Not for now at least. Let me think it over and devise a solution for your problem. I can see that your obsession is going to drive you farther away from your life which I will never let happen. Wait for me till the morning tomorrow." said Nadia briskly and left the room.

CHAPTER 10
A PLOT

I

Morning dawned harbouring a curious anxiety Ira had spent the night with. She had no clue on what Nadia was trying to work upon in her own capacity. But she had definitely meant something. Ira had seen that business like determination on her face last night. She trusted her well known efficiency in such matters where thinking was required. She knew, in affairs of head Nadia seldom faltered.

A little later Nadia entered her room with their faithful Damas. They both greeted the royal maiden and Damas addressed,

"The medicines which we shall require for our… our arrangement are already with us my Lady. I will go and prepare the Dhoarn-Aasrun (Dhatura and Tagar in hindi or Devil's Trumpet and Crape Jasmine in English) concoction in proper proportions. I will also carry out a test on one of my aides before we can use it on Aarya Manu. It will take just one day to come up with the results… that is the physical effects, if any. I will revert to you soon on all the developments once I have your permission to start the experiment."

Ira could not understand anything. Experiment with Dhoarn-Aasrun concoction? What of it? Those medicinal plants (mixed together as per specific methodical processes) were known to induce a complete memory loss for at least five-six months! And using it on Aarya Manu… Lord! What was Nadia planning to do?

"Experiment…? What do you…"she turned enquiringly at her companion friend who nodded in assertion. Ira signalled Damas out of her room to get details on the whole issue.

"Ira," Nadia said, "Since you were not prepared to listen to me I had to think after listening to you. If as you say nothing can be done about your feelings for the Manav King, we must think of working on it elsewise. Saving your life is my sole objective and I am going to see to it…. no matter how difficult you make it for me. So Ira, I propose that we temporarily relieve Aarya Manu of his memory, his people, his Manali and his Kamayani… albeit for a short period of time. Then we lure…no, actually abduct him to Causeruman."

Ira glared with exploding eyes in the horror of the idea!!

II

Tactfully bringing the Princess out from her initial inhibitions Nadia slowly explained to her the whole plot of stealing Manu from the people of Manali and from Kamayani.

As per the plan Manu was to be purposely injured by a (harmless) insect bite on route to one of his (which were quite frequent) visits to the lower banks of Arjikiya, following which Damas from Ira's camp was to appear for help. Faking the abrasive Dhoarn-Aasrun concoction as a medicinal treatment for the specific insect bite, they were to induce Manu into drinking it. Then they will kidnap a collapsed Manav King who would be made to wake up from his slumber only after 3-4 days. And once they reached Causeruman, it will be put to Ira and Shambar for getting him married!

Ira considered. She thought about the deviousness of the whole plot... She could see how unscrupulous the planning was. She perceived the immorality of the idea... To have an unsuspecting man kidnapped by deceit. She considered the injustice involved in inducing dementia to a perfectly healthy mind, and getting the man married off against his will or wishes!

However cleverly they might try to explain later, she could see how cunning everything was. And then she saw Manu... the charmer.

She saw a picture perfect Manu emerging out of that deception. As if superlatively sculpted by some other creator, she saw the handsome Manav King walk in his majestic stride towards her - smiling and looking at her. Manu, with his enchanting influences... Manu with his entrapping appeal... Manu with his enigmatic mesmerisms... coming to her, for her!

Ira saw Manu as she saw him that one night – dressed in a white wrap with a golden waistband, wearing the red head-dress...with a string of pearls attached to its side... and embraced in his long arms, bonded below his chin, soaked in his warmth wasn't Kamayani, it was Ira!!

Her body shivered with anxiety…. and her heart perspired. The thought of being close, so close to the man she loved filled her with a sensation yet unknown to her. She tightly closed her eyes to relish the prospect for a longer time. To be loved by Manu, engrossed in his arms, kissed by him…! Possible?

"… and then we are going to return him back to his place… to the Manavas, his people," Nadia was detailing, "after say, six months are over we will tell him our story. That is, about an insect bite which had a cure only at Causeruman. So we can say that we had no choice but to lift him and though cured of poison he had lost his memory temporarily as the aftereffect of treatment. Meanwhile some plausible explanation can be worked on, for organising the marital tie up between the two of you. It has to be in consultation with your father the King for marrying off his only daughter, you, to him. Or maybe something else…. but of course these are details we can see to later on when we reach our palace," Nadia had elaborated.

Ira was stumped. The whole plot appeared workable, at least up-till now. "And what will happen at the end of those five months or six? Will he like staying with me at Causeruman forever? No. I'm sure he will return here when he regains his memory. Then what becomes of me?"

"It will be up to him if he would like to stay there at Causeruman or return back to Manali – settling down with you and Kamayani both as his wives. The three of you – Manu, Kamayani and you Ira, can live happily ever after. He will no doubt return back to his land and his people when he regains his memory. But once he gets married to you he will be fair to you this is for sure. I know him that much too."

"..." Ira nodded.

"You can sort it out later among yourselves as per the situation demands. But for now at least this little deception needs to be staged. Well, think about it – this is not such a treacherous thing after all..." Nadia continued. She was, as if reading every thought that crossed her friend's mind clearly and she had all the answers ready for her.

"... You mean we will be acting selfish only for a short period of time? Then I... I eh, I should think I do not mind. But all this is not ethical... Is it Nadia?"

"No. It is not ethical. But let us come to face the facts here. There is no other way left for me to save you. Your life is my only and prime concern, and I'm going to see to its safety. So we are left with two options. One - either you are going with me back to Causeruman right now, and forget all about Manu and Manali..."

"No. I am not..."

"....then I do not see a choice. We go on with the plan I have thought of. Besides, I don't think there is any risk or a gross injustice involved. You will get what you want and he will be back into his own place after ....after whatever certain things are arranged between you and him. After all, the Manav King loses nothing."

"Y... yes. But are you certain Nadia...? You're sure he won't hate me once he regains his memory, say after six months?"

"Oh why will he? We are going to tell him that plausible story I just told you! And as I told you I know he is a sensitive man... he will never leave you once you two get married. Even when he regains his memory he will be nice to you. So don't worry on that aspect my dear."

"And your concoction? Is it a safe potion? He....he will not be harmed irreversibly?"

"Have no fear. This is a tried and tested potion. Completely reliable".

"Any physical implication?"

"None what-so-ever. Your Aarya Manu is going to be safe, healthy and fine. Trust Nadia for what I am doing. Ira, I know all of it sounds pretty complicated – but we can handle. It is actually amazingly simple and manageable. Everything will be fine in the end. I can see no other way left for us... and I have no better words to convince you."

Ira searched her friend's face thoroughly. Not a flick of hesitation, not a tinge of doubt sailed in her beady eyes. They were confident and unwavering. Believing in her conviction Ira finally tilted her head in approval.

Nadia called Damas inside for further scheming.

CHAPTER 11
THE ABDUCTION

I

It were more than two days since Manu left Manali.

That morning he had gone to see the Saptrishiganas[43] and he was travelling alone. He wanted to seek solace from his mentors as he was troubled at the sudden undesirable tangle of emotions the situations had dragged him in. Here he was, barely beginning to think about his personal happiness and all this complication with the foreign girl had cropped up. It had rummaged his mind with upsetting disturbances.

People at Manali knew their King would go alone to the Rishiganas for guidance whenever he was personally disturbed. He used to cross the river and walk up to the cliff where the sages meditated. It took him a day or maximum two to return - depending on the complexity of his query.

This time however Manu had taken a day more than required. The Manavas at Manali were anxious, and Kamayani was uneasy.

It had never happened earlier before. Manu used to be back within the time frame he had fixed for a particular mission. And this time not one but two

[43] A plural for Sage in Sanskrit (Rishi + Gana = Sage + folk)

additional days had lapsed which were definitely extravagant.

It wasn't like him at all – to go unscheduled this long without informing his people.

Kamayani was sensing something. Something amiss… out of ordinary. But what exactly was it there was no indication to it.

Uncertain to the cause Kamayani finally confided in Suvarna (her childhood friend, daughter of Vaayu – the Army chief) on the third morning. Suvarna too expressed her concern but still advised her to wait till another quarter of the day, 'he might be meditating there,' she had said.

They unrewardingly waited till the mid-noon to see Manu return. When not even a leaf turned up they decided to take it up with Prithu who was himself approaching Kamayani for a similar perplexity.

"Even I am wondering what made Aarya Manu stay back… he never does so," Prithu said thoughtfully, "though I know nothing can go wrong with him…" he had paused.

"Taat[44] Prithu, we should at least do something? It…I mean this is the third evening and we have no news, no message coming from Aarya Manu. This is very unusual, isn't it?" Suvarna pressed.

"Yes. That is so unlike him. And makes me little worried I admit… I think Som and Pawan (his two

[44] Respectful address for a fatherly figure

trusted aides) shall go and look out for him in the direction he went."

II

It was morning of the day four.

Som and Pawan had visited the Saptrishis' abode and they had found the seven Sages in deep Samadhi[45]. They knew therefore, Manu couldn't have been there. It was certain because no mortal being or anything could dare to disturb the great sages in their meditative state. No one could have come there – not even Manu.

If not here where was Manu since past three days?

Panicked for the first time now, Som and Pawan had searched fanatically for their King everywhere - beyond the river banks, over the cliffs, gorges, creeks, plains....they had spent the whole night calling out for him.

But in vain! Manu was nowhere to be found.

Broke and dismayed they had come back to Manali at dawn, wearing a forlorn look on their haggard faces. Prithu, Vayu, Dhriti, Kamayani and every single member of the whole community collected and sat thinking intently over Manu's unexplained disappearance. They had no clue on what was happening around their peaceful village Manali.

In the absence of their beloved leader Manu their wits seemed to have failed them - they were not sure

[45] A deep meditating condition when the person is fixed in one position – he doesn't move, eat, sleep or talk either.

what could they do now…initiate a search themselves, wait for some more time or they should call the Adityas or Yakshas[46] for help?

Suddenly Prithu remembered, "We can ask the visitors… the Causeruman people. Aarya Manu must have crossed Arjikiya from their campsite. Possibly someone from their side could have seen him?"

On an impulse Som and Pawan lifted their heads with a sudden comprehension. They exchanged glances between themselves,

"My God! Can it be? …could it be? But... is it possible?" Som said, not suppressing the alarm in his words.

"What is possible? Som, tell us what is it?" Prithu demanded.

"The Causeruman camp. It has vanished….gone!"

"Gone? You mean they've left? How… when? Without a word? Really? ....why?"

"But are you sure? Did you check around?" Vayu asked.

"There's not a feather flocking at the site, Arya Vayu!" Pawan retorted.

Kamayani was listening mutely up-till now, now she sank to the ground murmuring, "…so she took him" Suvarna rushed to hold her preventing her fall.

---

[46] Another Vedic era sub-divine community

III

The Manavas braved their shock and strains to gather themselves up for further thinking. After Kamayani divulged the Causeruman Princess's obsession and her dialogue with their King everyone was convinced of her being the reason behind Manu and the visitor camp's sudden disappearance. Suvarna added her observation on the day of celebrations when she had caught Ira gazing unblinkingly at Manu.

What they could fail to understand was, how a person of Manu's calibre could be abducted against his wishes?

They knew their leader's strength. He was practically invincible and couldn't possibly be intimidated by that miniature army of 8-10 Asuras. That ruled out, but wishfully why would Manu go with them without informing any of his people? Even that was not possible. It had to be some foul play....some underhand plot!

Their suspicions got firmer when someone from the crowd remembered how 'one of their men was probing Manu's movements a couple of days before he left'.

It was adjudged finally, that Manu was being carried away to Causeruman by some unfair means. Which way was it arranged or how could it happen was beyond their reasoning. The Manavas were a set of innocent people – their imagination could never have probed to the level Asuras had stooped to. The group had one respite though – the Causeruman Princess was in love with their King so she was going to keep him surely safe.

Kamayani's inner strength was put to test this time. Her people were to be held together, without a panic strike evident through her composure. It could result in further depression and chaos deflecting everyone's focus from need of the hour. Manu's pursuit required more attention than Kamayani's grievance.

They needed to sit together and think hard, really hard in order to secure their leader back safely. Kamayani displayed a depth befitting a Queen and contributed sensibly to the symposium,

"Is anyone here among us who knows where this place Causeruman could be?"

"....or any other thing, anything? About the place or the Asur people....maybe?" Prithu was observing the whole group's daunting silence on the subject.

Since nobody had an answer or any illuminating input, it was decided to seek immediate help available close at hand. But they remembered the great Saptrishis were in Samadhi. No one could disturb them in their meditation so they had to look beyond for guidance.

"The Adityas....! Mighty Adityas will know everything about this place and the people. We must at once reach out to them!" Aaryá Dhriti recalled.

She was right. A team of four Manavas at once left for Amaravati[47], Shakra's faraway city.

IV

It was at least a twenty plus five day affair – to reach Amaravati and come back at Manali after gathering the Adityas' support. But there was hardly a choice, for they could do nothing on their own.

Firstly they had no idea of the direction in which to launch their search. Secondly the valuable time lapse of initial four days had propelled them to think that by now their King's abductors might have gone well beyond their reach. They also had to consider the full strength of the Asuras (of which they had no actual assessment) vis-à-vis a set of oddly sixty (females excluded) Manavas – minus Manu, their tower of strength who was held captive by the Asuras.

The one thing Manavas could still not conceive of was the probability that had held Manu captive… there wasn't a soul under the sun who could use force on him! He was the best known warrior on the planet having an exceptional dexterity with his heavy sword which he used to carry tied to his waist whenever he went out. He had carried it that day also. No one could make him bow down with that blade in his hands… it wasn't possible.

Also apparently there were no suggestive marks on the site of the foreign pavilion that indicated struggle.

---

[47] A Vedic era city of Devas, believed to be somewhere near Mt. Kailash, closer to modern day kingdom of Nepal

But something had happened... there at the other side banks of Arjikiya some 'out of the ordinary' occurrence did take place. It was concluded so because of the sudden and un-informed departure of the campers. However, all the Manavas and Kamayani had the conviction of Manu's well-being in the wake of their culprit's passionate fascination for him. He will be kept favourably they knew.

Every moment at Manali went on to test the Manavas' forte. They were holding on to a treacherous optimism, their hearts lurking with an anguish within. They all seemed poised superficially by acting calm but they weren't quite. After all what were the Manavas without Manu?

CHAPTER 12

ON THE WAY TO CAUSERUMAN

I

The plot was supremely successful.

On the day when Manu set off from Manali to meet the Saptrishis, Damas had his men trail him. They threw a vicious looking but actually non-poisonous scorpion (which they carried from Causeruman into their medicinal tool box) at him. The insect stung his foot hard and Manu shrivelled in pain. Damas pretended to be passing by, and checking the grievance advised the Manav King an ïmmediate anti-dote for the "dangerous" poison.

A completely unsuspecting Manu went up to the Causeruman camp, drank the strange concoction....and collapsed into deep slumber in no time.

Necessary preparations were already thorough and the visitors had immediately left carrying their prized catch as per their shrewd planning. Much before anyone could notice they were on their track - back to the Asur territory of Shambarasur. Casually inquiring from Manavas about Manu's travel plans, the campers had beforehand ensured that no one was going to notice Manu's absence for at least a couple of days lest they run the risk of being followed. So far so good.

II

The Asur girls got rid of Manu's sword in one of the several rivers they had crossed. A latent, defenceless and unarmed Manu lay unconscious in the waggon. Ira had ensured his comfort by piling up her most comfortable rugs under him.... she herself was travelling in the same carriage to be near him and keep a vigil on his helpless body. Nadia the master planner companion sat by her side.

Ira didn't like to see the illustrious Manav King lie that way - reliant, motionless, inert. But it had to be so because there was no other way she could fancy her having a chance to be so close to him. 'Once he wakes up he will see only me... and forget all about Kamayani', she had said to herself repeatedly as she kept admiring the serene charm of the sleeping man. It was as if a child enjoying having acquired the bauble she had cried for.

"We can make him wake up once we descend the Himalayas, umm....Nadia?" Ira asked.

"Oh yes. It is only a day and a half since we are travelling. And with the kind of speed our Damas is manoeuvring the Caravan, we shall be crossing the plains of Saraswati by tomorrow evening. After that when we reach Sindhu we can make him wake up. To be safe I think, morning after the morrow."

"Nadia, how would you answer if I asked you one thing?"

"What is it?"

"His people, the Manavas were so kind to us. Even Kamayani treated us so well. And yet we.... actually I... have done this to them! I stole their Man in the worst possible manner. I am beginning to..."

"Regret? Do you regret... you want to retreat? If you want to have second thoughts, we can surrender him back to his people. There is still time..."

"No... not regret. I didn't mean to retreat. Not after I know... Oh! I can feel what it is like being so close to him. Aarya Manu is my life Nadia. I can see him, touch him, be near him... And I know now that I'd do anything in the world for this! Yet I admit being very, very unfair to Kamayani and those Manav people. I am beginning to think that I could be... eh, I could be remembered for setting the wrong precedents for all the people in love. I may never be forgiven by history. Do you also feel the same? Do you think I should have spent my whole life crying my heart out for Aarya Manu instead of using this... e different sort of clever strategy?"

"Well! ....well, you have something there. But I guess we have to see it in a slightly different light. If you were able to I would advise you to forget all about him and just go back to your own land. But you said you could not think of living without Aarya Manu. If I let you die... which you would eventually knowing your passion, I would be risking many more lives back home.

Your father the Great Shambar will certainly find life difficult seeing you go through the torture you were prepared to be subjecting to yourself. All the Asuras depend so much… I should say solely on your father. How wise can it be putting a whole race's survival at stake for an unfortunate one sided emotion you had developed? I also had to consider many other people who live to see you happy and alive… not sobbing away to death.

And why? What for …when all this could be taken care of through some intelligent thinking and seamless planning? So why not! I opine that everyone needs to weigh their selfishness at times. On one side is only one person getting deceived and on the other - a whole race's survival. Besides we are not setting any wrong precedents as we will eventually return him to his original space, his own place and people including his wife. And our arrangement doesn't take away anything from anyone… we are just trying to add things."

"As you say we might be trying to add things, by being… calculatedly selfish?"

"Oh Ira forget it now will you!" Nadia was irritated. Ira was being really difficult now. She knew things as they stood – right and wrong shouldn't bother her at a time when she had already carried her afflictions this far.

"Right. I will not think about it anymore. I know I am being selfish… I will be, for the sake of Aarya Manu. I can be, for I too have a right to live… and love. As for Kamayani and the Manavas I will rectify it up for them when my term ends – after six months." Mused Ira.

Thus the two girls debated among themselves and self-adjudicated their actions. Having found their thinking suitable they did not care to consider the ethics. Nor did they consider the turmoil Manu's feelings were going to undergo… being churned in a transient amnesia, and a subsequent recovery amidst which he was going to be married off to someone he couldn't love. And the pain, the anguish of being separated from his love, his people, his own land for which he had strived so hard!

But such insensitive was the Asur girl's inclination, and it had to be fixed equally insensitively… like this.

SECTION III

AT THE STONE CASTLE

CHAPTER 13

A NEW NAME AND A NEW GAME

I

Manu had mostly slept throughout the journey or he merely kept calm struggling inwards to relocate his memory. He had awaken but his faculties were weak owing to the regulated dosage of the strange concoction which was administered to him on the pretext of being the medicine for a highly poisonous insect bite.

One day when he was utterly baffled trying to remember his name at least, he had asked the girls travelling with him (not in the same cart since when he was awake) about his name.

"What… could be my name Shubhe, if you know? I seem to have forgotten even that",

"Mmm… a…nu…" Ira had mumbled, but was quickly taken over by Nadia, "…nu… eh… eh," she coughed artificially.

"Nu… Nueh…?" asked Manu.

"N… eh… eh. No… Noah… you, your name is Noah. I think that's what those villagers told us. They could not possibly have a cure for the scorpion that stung you so we had to hurry bringing you along with us. When we reach Causeruman your proper medication will start. You will be fine and gradually regain your memory also." Nadia had said hurriedly.

II

Manu's captors landed safely inside the boundaries of their region. They had carried a half-dazed, a muddled Manav King as some precious bag of possession for their Princess.

After speeding through the uninhabited terrain for nearly fifteen days the Caravan had reached the outpost of Causeruman, and crossing over ***Beyond the stone-hedge*** they were soon in to Shambarasur's stone castle finally.

Shambar was rejoiced to see his daughter back after so many months. He was eager to speak to her at length, but the girl had quietly entered her private chambers leaving all the talking for Nadia to do.

The story we know as happened up till now was disclosed to the Asur King by Nadia. Was he angry at the peculiar turn of events planned and executed by the two girls, or did he approve of his daughter's infatuation with the Manav King Manu, or was he worried about the retaliation expected by the Manavas - one cannot actually say. For he had said nothing, save for after listening to the whole story through Nadia's distinctly clear narrative he merely shook his head several times and said,

"Whatever has happened, has happened. There's no use trying to adjudicate. And how well do I know – it is in our blood....inviting trouble from just about nowhere. So be it. Tell Ira to come to me tomorrow morning."

III

Ira stood in front of her father prepared to face his unpredictable temper the next day. She knew Nadia had explained everything to him but she didn't know of his reactions.

Nevertheless she had appeared at his chamber in time. Because being fearlessly defensive of their actions was one of the most prominent Asur trait!

The Asuras lived with altogether different codes than the likes of Manavas or Adityas. They were not in the habit of judging their actions. Their society had never known any directives, morality margins or conduct confines. They were brought up learning to get what they wanted. Shambar himself had married forcibly without being sensitive to know his partner's (Ira's mother) will or wish. Ira too had it in her blood.

Hesitantly she had told him whatever she could, of her inability to think beyond the Manav King and of the strange desire punishing her heart ever since she saw Manu. Shambar had listened patiently. Then he drew a deep breath and said,

"Hmm. Yeah, maybe I know. We Asuras are made that way. Once we want a thing, we want it. I know because I am myself that way. Ideally you should have married Banasur and settled happily thereafter but no... that won't do for you. In fact it has always been like this for us. When we have our lives perfectly settled and are living in peace, we look out for trouble elsewhere and handhold it to come to us. Our history is loaded with numerous examples. Anyhow, these blasted Manavas... may the Lord curse them for being alive... I haven't heard of such a community. And the way you tell me, they appear to be quite a force - I do not expect them to sit quietly over the loss of their leader."

Ira started nervously "But father, I... we...Nadia made sure that..."

"There...there do not fret. You do not have to worry. I, your father the Great Shambarasur is here to take care of such matters. So go on child, do not fret. Prepare your Manu... Noah or whatever he is, to get married to you quickly before any trouble from their side comes up."

Sending Ira back to her own concerns Shambar thought solemnly about the whole episode. 'Well... not too bad at all... Shradhhdev Manu - the erstwhile Prince of Aaryavart[48], son of the greatest King Surya! Of course I know the name... I have known his father. If he is to be my son-in-law I will be more secure. And assured from the Adityas' side. Surya and Shakra were great friends so I recognize, and it will be beneficial to earn Shakra's proximity in this fashion. May be even the age old rivalry from the times of Madasur can get dissolved! Good job there, the girl has been excellent in her choice!' Shambar was actually smiling.

But there was another problem he was likely to face soon - the Manavas. Who were these people who had

[48] Indian subcontinent

been living under Manu's leadership? What were they like... or how were they temperamentally? He had never heard of them. May be someone who had travelled deeper into Brahmavart could know. But none of his subjects belonged to that region... nobody ever heard of such a community.

Then who were these confounded people? Where did they spring up from, all of a sudden? And that strange place with a stranger name... Manavi... or was it Manaki? Who could have heard of this Himalayan village...? Himalayan? But of course...! Banasur! Banasur came treading along the Himalayas... he will know something if not all. Shambar summoned Banasur immediately to his chamber.

IV

By Now Banasur had heard the whole account (broadly) from Damas. He could not believe his luck – Manu? Again the same Manu after all these years? Emerging out of nowhere from a far off horizon, again seizing everything Banasur had hoped for! Yet again the same Manu... how could it happen to him?

Banasur was fuming. He wanted Ira so badly. He even forsake his title, 'Asur King Banasur' for her! He was living submissively under the gumshoe of another Asur as his military general merely because he wished to marry his daughter someday.

Marrying Ira would have inevitably made him heir to the throne, making everything come around to him finally. And today when he was almost slated to achieve his feat, this obnoxious Manu suddenly appears and takes away whom? Ira? His, Banasur's own ambition Ira! How could he? And Shambar? What has been the matter with him… how could he disregard Bana's contributions to his kingdom so easily as to allow Ira to bring Manu here as her chosen man? Banasur bit his lips and was mad with rage. He will make them all pay for it! Each one of them!

Bana received Shambar's summons and saw him in his consulting room. He told Shambar the story of Manu, Manavas and Manali. Having informed of the history of Manu and Manavas[49] Shambar now saw the danger lurking on his Causeruman kingdom. Certainly there was danger.

"It means," said he, "That we have collectively invited the wrath of Adityas, Marutas and Vasus against us. They will not take long to find us even without the Saptrishis helping them. I know the whole lot well. The ninth Aditya[50] Savita has the reputation of being an excellent explorer. He has an amazing knowledge of global geography, and is sure to find the shortest possible route to Causeruman without a help. I say we have to be prepared now Banasur, for although we will try to avoid at all costs but there might be another Aditya-Asur battle on the cards."

"Absolutely my great King. If you permit me I want to erect a post – a cantonment with sturdy stone bastions to stop them midway. Much before they can reach our

---

[49] Ref : The Book 'From Zero To One – the Story Of Manu' by MVG (Maneesha Agrawal)

[50] They were twelve, Shakra, the leader, Dhaata, Bhag, Tvashta, Mitra, Vivasvan, Varun, Yam, Savita, Poosha, Anshuman, and Jishnu

Causeruman boundary. I can see to it that… you must leave it to me." Bana said. He turned away with eyes blazing with accumulated anger. '…even I have a few scores to settle with the league. I would raise my own loyal army at the cantonment in order to deal with Manu's men and then Shambar later, once I get the Manavas fixed,' he was thinking in his heat.

Shambar agreed to do what his supreme commander had suggested. He was not much pleased with his daughter's doing now that he knew the Manavas… none other than the very famous Shakra's ex-army-men! Add to it the valiant Vasus… how perilous it could turn out to be if they all fought against the Asuras together! It was no use fighting them at all. Maybe Nadia's story of a poisonous insect bite would help…

Shambarasur despatched Banasur along with half of his army at a midway post that stood at the outskirts of his stone citadel. The army quickly got busy with preparations. They were constructing an outpost with huge boulders to apprehend enemy progression the moment they spotted any.

CHAPTER 14
THE MARRIAGE

I

Ira was thoughtful. She and Nadia could not find a way or a pretext to introduce their big idea of marriage to Manu (now Noah). They had to think of something worthwhile, as Manu was likely to retain these memories later when he would finally recover and recall everything. Hence everything had to look fair and rational. What could be the possibility of a stranger getting married to a Princess?

"A... a Swayamvar[51]? Yes....! How about a Swayamvar? The traditional and simplest way. I will choose Aarya Manu in front of all our people present in a specially called assembly... he will be confused, but he won't refuse. We will not give him a chance to refuse. What do you think?" Ira exclaimed.

"Excellent. This will work just the way we want. We will make sure that he is present in the assembly... and be careful not to let him know of the reason behind the gathering. Otherwise he may not attend. Another precaution we must observe is that he shouldn't know as per our Asur traditions mutual exchange of garlands is the only ritual necessary for solemnizing a marriage.... we must use this fact to our benefit."

---

[51] A practice in ancient India where the girl chooses her life partner on her own out of an assembly of invitees.

"Yes? ...why? And how?"

"You must ensure that he doesn't know anything about your idea. Nor should he know that he is actually getting married with the garlanding procedure. Remember that we have to keep him in dark till you are able to befriend him better."

"Now why and how am I going to manage this? That sounds like a complicated chain of quite unnecessary secrets..." the Princess was frowning at the unattractive idea.

"Just tell him it is not an actual wedding, only some preliminary announcement and nothing much."

"....oh but why?"

"...because if he gets to know later that he was deceitfully married off like this without his consent, you will find it very difficult to justify the complete sequence at the end of six months."

"Eh... okay... yes. Okay, if you say so." Ira shrugged her shoulders.

"We will invite him at the assembly through your Father. There when once you garland him in front of so many people, his chivalry will not let him step back[52]. We will think of a simple reason as explanations for the time being." Nadia suggested.

---

[52] Because as per the prevalent customs those days, if a girl garlanded someone in a Swayamvar, she was labelled to be his wife whether he liked it or not. She wasn't accepted by anyone else then

"Exactly. Great! This sounds good. So you go to Father right now and ask him to announce my Swayamvar next week whichever day he finds suitable. Next week because I think Aarya Manu's physical and mental conditions need at least that much of rest to be better. I will also speak to Father in this regard today evening." Settled Ira.

My God! The way these two girls were scheming and conspiring with an amazing accuracy.... Who would have known such traits to be present in those innocuous hearts with such innocent faces! But O' seething desire! O' frantic passion! What cannot thy do? When you burn the core, unrestrained commissions are dealt with - in the canniest of ways by the simplest of minds.

II

The Causeruman people were present in their full strength at the court square to witness the Swayamvar of their Princess Ira. Manu (or Noah) was present in the assembly as he was requested to attend 'a certain ceremonial procession' announced by the Asur King Shambar.

Manu was staying at the guest quarters of the castle. He was under the 'observation and medication' of a royal doctor. A physically very weak Manu has had no respite from his much frequent slumber, and all those perplexing mental concussions which were making him weaker every day. He was not eating or resting properly.

Manu was regularly visited by Ira whom he recognized as his saviour and a gentle, kind friend. But to his dismay whenever Manu had attempted to question her about his identity or his antecedents (now completely oblivious to him), Ira would look at him with worried eyes – as if trying to keep something away. This often made Manu wonder, 'do I carry a past that is forgettable?' To this his heart said no – always a very emphatic no.

His heart kept telling him that it had a vibrancy alive inside… some exuberance which was as compelling as not ready to subside… an animation was pulling upon him to believe… Ah what? After all, what?

No announcement was done prior to the Princess's arrival as was the customary practice in a Swayamvar because according to the plan Manu was to stay unaware of their real intent. At the pre-set hour Ira appeared in the assembly. Dressed in one of her finest draperies and diamonds she looked resplendent in her flowery peach and pink costume. Her golden hair shone with a brilliance that even her fair face wore today. She felt divine - she was going to marry her man, her Manu finally.

Being wife to the best of all mortals, the finest man on this earth was something that doesn't happen to everyone. She would be his wife from now. She will be as distinguished as Kamayani… and even make a place in Manu's heart someday soon. Her heart was vibrating with a vigour she had not experienced before and her lips were twitching continuously, failing to contain their smile. What a moment it was for her! Too ecstatic to be believed real.

Another Asur girl walked by the Princess with a garland hung on her forearm (Ira didn't hold it herself purposely as per the planning).

Escorted by Shambar and Nadia, Ira had all eyes glued to her today. Her charm had increased with the peach and pink emotions colouring her countenance.

But for the man in question it was a curiosity rather than any admiration. Manu was entirely detached and watched the whole set of proceedings without a real interest. So many curious customs and ceremonies take place every day in this strange vast world, he might have been thinking.

The Princess walked straight towards Manu who was seated in the first row and before he could realize what was happening to him, Ira slid a garland onto his neck! The crowds suddenly went ecstatic cheering "Noah! Noah! Noah! .....".

Shambar as if initially surprised, hesitated, waited, embraced and then hugged Manu tight.

'What... on earth does this mean? Oh Lord! What is going on??' An agonizingly confused Manu saw - Shambar held Manu's arm in one hand and his daughter's in the other...

Raising both their hands up he made a loud announcement, "here is my daughter's chosen husband Noah. I declare him my son and heir to my throne henceforth. So people, come let's greet and welcome Noah to Causeruman..."

The rowdy Asur crowd roared. They screamed and shouted unwaveringly, expressing their delight at the King's announcements. Amidst that hullabaloo Manu stood astounded. He was speechless... thunderstruck, staggered as if traversing from a bad to a worse dream...

CHAPTER 15

MANU AT CAUSERUMAN

I

Ira and Manu were led to a new, a little inordinately decked up chamber into the stone castle that evening. It was tastefully lit up with coloured wax candles, and huge vases of perfumed flowers stood in pairs.

For a person already struggling with psychological irregularities, the strange enactment at the castle's court square proved exceedingly strenuous for Manu. He was not in his complete control but still he was Manu – the best among mortals. He knew something unbecoming was happening around him. As if he was the nucleus of some weird, treacherous whirlwind proceedings spun around him. He strained his cerebral faculty... trying to perceive, trying to understand, to regain something. But it was to no avail.

Ira's delight knew no boundaries today. She had achieved what she had set out to. After days of continued suffering her moment was finally here. She was Manu's wife from this day.

Manu... the man who was the pride of Manavas and life of Kamayani. The iconic hero Manu who was every girl's dream man... The young, handsome, suave, charismatic Manav King Manu was with Ira today.

Today he was her Manu… sitting in her chamber as her husband and the declared heir to her father's kingdom. What else could life give her…. She'll stay with him forever now. Ira looked eagerly at her prized catch who sat frowning. He was tensed and absolutely adrift.

"Aary… No, a… Noah, are you not happy?"

"Happy? You cannot be serious Shubhe, you must… First tell me what was it that happened today?"

"Nothing out of ordinary." She had tried to sound very casual, "My father was searching for an heir to this vast kingdom of Causeruman as he doesn't have a son. He could never like any of the Asuras here. But he took a liking to you when you came here. So he has selected and announced you as the next ruler for his subjects. That's all that has happened today. "

"Really? But why? And the …the sudden…" he pointed to the garland in his neck, "This?"

"Oh yes this. It is our tradition. If a stranger or a non-Asur has to be our King, he has to marry someone within the community to be able to belong here. Then Father consulted me on finding a suitable bride for you. And I… well I think he thought I was the best maiden around. So…so…"

"…but you should have asked me at least… don't you think? And why such an urgency to choose the heir right now?"

"Yes I should have asked you, ideally. But looking at your condition I did not feel I ought to have given you any added strain. And those declarations could not wait, Noah, for… umm… the…" Ira was trying to dodge the question of urgency, till she could think of an answer.

"Declarations? Then it wasn't …"

"…a marriage? No. Of course not. There wasn't actually a wedding taking place. It was just a kind of announcement we had the urgency to make. The… rituals and other things can be finalized later on whenever you feel comfortable." She lied as she couldn't think faster.

"Oh but why you had to do so immediately... now in the first place?" Manu persisted as he was still failing to see a reason.

Ira hesitated and then it came. Thinking quickly she added, "E… I will tell you. We had a prediction from the royal astrologer forecasting an imminent Dev[53]- Asur battle soon. Therefore we needed a royal heir immediately as is our custom to declare the next King before something untoward happens in a battlefield. And father doesn't see anyone worthy of wielding such a responsibility among his existing lot. They are all so reckless. Then you came… and you were so different – extraordinary. He… in fact we all liked you for the role. So you see this had to be arranged pretty quickly. But for now you should forget all of this… will you? These are issues that hold no importance right now. You must

[53] The Adityas

have proper rest and take care of your own condition. The poison seems to have been very hazardous...." Ira rolled the conversation on some other track and left a bewildered Manu somewhat convinced, somewhat unimpressed!

II

Two more mornings came and went by and the new couple at Causeruman was ill at ease. Manu, because he was unwilling to submit to the circumstances which were being presented to him. He had largely regained his physical strength but his mental confusions had apparently multiplied by the somewhat dubious explanations given to him on the sudden, odd turn of events. For they were odd.

He wandered in and about the palace (shadowed secretly by Shambar's men), thinking hard while trying to correlate his heart's feelings and mind's readings. There was a continuous conflict - his brain wasn't clear with anything but the heart said something was wrong somewhere in the whole set-up. Things were not as they appeared. His sharp mind could feel that it was all wrong. Adding to his confusions was his hazy intellect. Retention of certain delineations from his past floated there. He could sense an awakening close-by, some past was there - struggling to resurge. But what?

As a result he kept mostly to himself avoiding everyone from the household including Ira. Since his imposed 'wedding announcement' with her he had purposely avoided Ira. They had continued to stay in their separate rooms in wake of keeping the whole deception under the wraps as was argued and settled between Ira and Nadia previously.

Princess Ira was uneasy as her man was still not hers' despite all those efforts. Whatever she had been thinking while she was planning and plotting was certainly not this. It wasn't turning out to be as easy and simple as she had imagined. She could see that another ordeal had actually begun for her now - to be in love with someone, be near him... and have your heart wrung when he stared blankly at something past behind you!

Ira had loved a captivating, energetic and agile human being who was in full charge of his and even other people's capacities. She had loved an influential personality who had the aura... the effect to induce passionate vitality in the eyes of an onlooker. She wanted to be in his arms... which were full of strength zeal and warmth. She had to feel the privilege of her being loved by Manu... resting her head enviably on his secure chest, the same way she had seen Kamayani do.

A beleaguered, sceptical, uneasy and distraught Manav King was not the Manu whom she had imagined loving her. Ira never hoped to see Manu like this. She felt broke, and confided in Nadia one evening,

"Nadia, it is all my fault my doing. It... it hurts beyond words to see him like this. He is struggling hard, oh so hard! I feel more and more responsible for this. Look at his over-wrought trauma Nadia! I... I shouldn't have done this to him... Really! I shouldn't have. You know how I feel seeing him in such excruciating pain? I would die Nadia... I will perish seeing him struggle like this one day… I… oh what do I do now… I must do something ….Please tell me anything that I can do. I have to…! Else I'll go mad. Why… he has never smiled even once all these days! All because of me…"

"Gather yourself dear… Stop! Hold on… there… there!" calmed Nadia. She held the sobbing Princess and placated her outburst tenderly, "Listen to me now… there."

Ira sobbed as Nadia said, "Imagine yourself, Ira, in a situation when you can't remember a one single day from your life. Let us say, yesterday. Your memory has no record of anything that you did or said yesterday. And then out of the blue a stranger turns up telling you that you had married him yesterday! How are you likely to receive the news? Tell me…?"

"Me? Why…I will never… eh…?" Ira gave a start. Lifting her head she looked at her friend…

"Exactly." Said Nadia, "it is not an easy situation to deal with. Give him time. What you want from him is not going to happen in a flash… It is a test of your patience and his bearings. You have a role here. You have to… to commiserate. Comfort him, soothe him, shrink his solitude, befriend him… Then maybe you can make him come closer to you. Remember Ira, he is Manu – the best among mortals. A highly intelligent and sharp human being. You or me cannot fabricate his feelings or manipulate his psyche… We can be suggestive at the most."

CHAPTER 16
PREDICAMENTS

I

Ira sat by the side-seat in her room. Manu was seated on the bed. The chilly winds of Causeruman had abandoned the room after a fire was lit up in the grate kept in one corner. Today Ira had caught up with him before he could go on his after-dinner evening walk.

The wintery evening had graduated into a frosty night and Ira was watching Manu stealthily from the corners of her big round eyes.

By now she had earned his friendship so that Manu did not make an attempt to evade her company whenever they were together. He regarded her as a coeval friend and often shared his confusions and visions that his diminished, but alive memory offered him. Ira listened to him and pretended to help but was cautious not to let him go closer to those glimpses. She tried to talk to him, largely shifting his attentions to various other things – the weather, the people, the Asur customs, practices, stories and day-to-day happenings at Causeruman, to keep him more engrossed there with herself. But did she succeed?

Today they had been to a local fete on her insistence and Ira had picked up some jewellery articles for herself. She had tried to make Manu interested in shopping for her and had inevitably failed. It was more than thirty days now since their wedding and she was still vying for her husband's elusive attention.

She stole a glance at him in the warm golden light whisking in the room. His pensive face looked very attractive…

"Noah…"

Manu attended with his usual reserved expression. He sat facing the fire, and the vibrant colours of flames ran through him… delicately drenching his subtle valour in a mesmerizing tinge. It had a disturbing effect on the besotted maiden.

"Look at these earrings Noah… the ones I bought today from the fete. Tell me, do they suit me fine?" She posed holding the danglers close to her ears.

"Yes they are good." said he, without looking.

"Noah…" Ira rose from her chair and sat kneeling in front of him, "Will you never, ever look at me?" Her tone pleaded and searched his eyes…

The desperation in the voice made Manu see her… Her golden hair rolled over her shoulders despondently and her white face flushed… colouring coming up revealing some deep penetrating twinge.

He saw, her sapphire blue eyes were lined with big tears wriggling to escape. He saw Ira probably for the first time today… He didn't know, that here was a heart which was burning every moment with desire…. Or that here were a pair of eyes which were pining every day with passion! How would he know, the severity of the draw he had been exerting on her? Something pulled a chord somewhere and he shut his eyes…

With closed eyes Manu saw a dream. He had a glimpse – a flicker of a white wrap, a red dot, a flower - a white lotus… All soaked in white moonlight. It was so peaceful so serene. For the first time he felt tranquil - a mental concord. All the fiery effects he was surrounded with (at that moment into Ira's room) were subdued… they had submerged into that serene silvery sparkle. He saw someone coming … And he jerked open his eyes saying "It isn't you…no, not you", and walked out of the room in the dead solitude of that moonless night.

CHAPTER 17
A MOVE

I

Ira was surprised to receive her Father's call early in the morning. 'It could be something to do with my Noah not attending the assembly regularly. Naturally Father might be expecting things now that a whole month has gone past. I will have to explain to him that he must be given some more time,' she was thinking.

She saw Shambar sitting on his gigantic rock throne. He looked vexed. Ira started,

"Father, I can explain... Noah will come around surely. Once I am able to convince him that he is loved and respected here as a leader I can tell you that he will be willing to pick-up. And he's really good. He will prove himself worthy but you must give us a few more..."

"Ira! Ira stop... will you? We have a bigger problem, child. They I mean his people... they are on his track. His men will be here any day to take him away. By now they have advanced in their crusade against us so I've come to know. And if I am correct which I believe I am, those choleric raiders will not be slow. I wish they all went to hell but they will reach here at Causeruman within a... let's say another twenty days!" the King grunted loudly.

He had received the news from a hoard of nomadic shepherds who had noticed an army marching somewhere around the Sindhu – Saraswati valley. The shepherds had conveyed the message to the outpost Banasur was holding, and from there it had reached the King.

Shambarasur was not keen on fighting with the collective forces of Adityas, Marutas and Vasus. It was suicidal he knew. He was thinking on some alternative strategy. For a first time in his life he wanted to avoid a war as long as he could, especially after knowing their backgrounds from Banasur. The Asur King Shambar was clearly stressed.

Ira trembled. She shook her head and cried, "But I will not let anyone take him away from me! Not at any cost!"

"Look I know what you feel. But it is true my girl. I suggest that you and your fellow should shift to Brazant[54] Giri[55] for at least a few days. You must realize how serious the issue is. You understand… what if we keep your fella… this Noah here and someone from his group sneaks in to meet him… Then? Or let's say he moves out and meets someone by chance? We will not be able to handle such situation. I say it is better to keep him out of any soul's reach." Waving his hands impatiently he continued, "…and to be honest I can't trust my own men with all this. They might be already having a grudge against him. We cannot let the situation

[54] Modern day Mt. Elbarus – the highest point of Caucasus.(the name Elbarus is derived from Iranian word Brazant, a modification of Sanskrit word 'Brihant' which means high)
[55] Sanskrit word for mountain

go out of control… you better take him away for a few days and leave me in peace. Let me think over the matter coolly. No one shall know except for a few close people."

Ira was stunned. She could not think of what to say. She may had been very shrewd in planning for her union with Manu… but for the repercussions she was definitely short of ideas.

"Go now Ira, and make your preparations early. Of course, take Nadia along too. I will see whatever I have to do." said her father.

As Ira turned to leave Shambar called from behind, "send Nadia to me at once…"

II

Nadia was standing quietly in the assembly hall presently occupied exclusively by Shambar and her. The Asur King asked her to relate the whole story once again - right since the day they (Ira's Caravan) had landed in Manali till date. He listened carefully word by word account of the plan of abduction, the execution and everything.

"Eh… that was indeed very clever of you Nadia. But not quite wise when it comes to thinking of this aftermath now… No. No I can't blame you even as I know my daughter. She is indeed gentle but has inherited the same obstinate Asur bolshiness in good proportions. Once we have an eye for a thing, we have it. She would either have her man – this blasted Noah or die… if not kill! Eh!"

"Tell me girl," said he, "this poison story you cocked up… what is the chance that anyone should doubt it? I mean does anyone know of it? Or has anyone seen anything?"

"No master. No one knows anything except for me and Damas. And no soul could have seen us - of this I can be very sure."

"Right. Good. Now listen to me carefully, and tell me if I sound believable or not. I shall send a welcoming contingent to the Adityas when they reach Bana's outpost. With a message that will say, 'your King is here with us. He had a dangerous scorpion or snake or whatever damn thing stinging him… following which my people had to lift him to Causeruman for proper treatment. You weren't informed because our Princess panicked seeing him that way and had left off in a hurry.' How does it sound to you? Plausible?"

"E… Yes. I think so. If we can add, 'and now that he has recovered, we were about to send him back at Manali with absolute regard. He is currently having a temporary amnesia from which he will soon recover and this is the reason we haven't been able to send him back up-till now.' Then I really do not think the Manavas or the Adityas will doubt it too much. Unless…"

"…yes?"

"…unless they know of the marriage!"

"The marriage…!"

"Yes my King. The moment we tell them about his sudden marriage with Ira they – especially Shakra or Prithu may see through the whole plot. Because there is a possibility that Kamayani had known and told them about Ira's fixation for her husband."

"Hmm…I see your point." said Shambar.

He waited a few seconds to think it over then resumed, "And if no one from our side tells them about this… the marriage, how are they likely to know?"

"Ira. Since she is bent upon staying with him she has to reveal it. And then of course Aarya Manu. He will remember whatever has been happening here with him. Although he still does not know conclusively that he has actually been married… I made Ira do so foreseeing such a situation. "

"Excellent. So let us continue to keep this fellow… Noah or Manu or whatever damn name he is… in dark. You take care of Ira and I will handle rest of my people. If I send our good Damas also at the outpost for placating the raiders, and not let the Adityas or Manavas come here… no one shall ever know the real story. And then I can personally go there with Noa… Manu to return him to his own crazy people. This sounds more convincing."

"I hope it will be so Master." said Nadia and left the room after a dismissal from the King.

The same evening Ira, Manu and Nadia (and a few other confidantes) were sent packing. The hideout was secluded heights of Brazant Giri. It was established to be doing good to the disturbed condition of the royal heir Noah, at least so was Manu told.

CHAPTER 18
AT BRAZANT GIRI

I

"No Nadia this won't do!" exclaimed Ira.

She and her wise companion were trying to argue upon a point. They had come to the freezing heights of Brazant Giri as per Shambarasur's instructions. Although it had snowed severely a couple of days ago, they were comfortable staying at a nicely warmed-up lodging prepared there for the royal heiress.

Four uneventful days had gone past increasing Ira's irritability and insecurity. She was trying to convey to her friend that she could not and will not, at no cost, let Manu go with the Manavas… without her. She like a child, was intractably stamping her feet and protesting against keeping her marriage under the wraps for a long (now apparently infinite) time!

"If I do not find a way to tell him that we are married as per our customs why will he take me along? Can't you see Nadia, it will be such a waste of everything we have done up till now. And… and why don't you understand that he is now my wedded husband. I am his wife. I need to…"

"….will you stop crying and try to hear my voice Ira?"

"No. I will not. You listen to me..! And for once YOU do just as I say…" screamed the Princess.

II

The initial pleasure Ira had at the thought of enjoying a secluded getaway with the man of her dreams had subsided sooner than expected. Manu was quieter now. He could afford to remain detached from his absolute environment including Ira here.

His efforts at recollection of memories from his life were disbursing slowly in the form of hazy hallucinations - albeit tediously, torturing his composure. But he was Manu, best of all mortals. He possessed a composition - a character which stimulated him to fight against the odds every time his mettle was put to test.

Keeping entirely to himself in the cold calmness of Brazant Giri he was struggling every minute to evoke his memories and to trust his own faculties. He roamed about in muted wilderness avoiding interactions, company, and sometimes even his supper. In the process he was a shade paler and weaker – apart from being tired mentally.

Within a few days the best of all mortals, the first King of Manavas, the superlative human being our agile Manu was exhausted and overtly tired.

III

Ira had asked Nadia to arrange for a white wrap and a few white flowers. She had distinctly remembered her first meeting with the Manav King when he was fetching white lilies (obviously for his wife - Ira judged) from the river.

She would entrap Manu, if not attract him today. She had made up her mind for this impish resolve as her patience had given up after thinking over and over again the news her father had given to her. The Manavas were marching to get Manu back… take him away from Ira. Soon he will be far beyond her reach and she might never see him again? Oh! She could not let it happen… at no cost!

Manu must take her along…

Whenever he was to leave Causeruman she will go with him. But why would he take her, if according to Shambar's wishes he does not know of his marriage with Ira? Her father was not ready to reveal the marriage for the fear of inviting the Aditya's wrath. Manu who had been trusting her as a friend till now may also start resenting her if he comes to know of the deception (of marriage) staged at the Asur court that day. Therefore the marriage could not be revealed.

Then what? There wasn't much time to think. Lord! She had to do something… something quick and definite.

'Only if…,' thought she, 'if…if I make him… involved somehow,' rose the desire in the grab of an option.

The romance brewing in Ira's heart had grieved severely seeing the injury inflicted to the man she loved.

It was a thwarting mixture of feelings she was reeling under – anxiety, apprehension, sorrow, remorse and above all, desperation!

Ira was an ordinary girl. She was an average Asur Princess who was fervently in love with an extraordinary man. She had already been through so much that her nuances were hardly capable of handling. Her desire, her yearning had played enough with her forbearance with no accomplishment – no success up-till now.

But the want wasn't diminishing. Each failure had in fact escalated the coveted craving… so much so that unable to bear her burdens Ira decided to write an episode for herself – the episode of treachery, fraudulence and vice!

CHAPTER 19

THAT ONE NIGHT

I

Nadia arranged everything as per Ira's instructions. She had cautioned the Princess against the whole idea as she did not think it was 'absolutely necessary'. There were other ways which could be thought upon, she had said. Plus there was the risk of her getting wounded in a worse way. But then Ira! The child-like, impulsive Ira! And her aching desire!

II

The night was obscurely opaque. It had cloaked one of those very strange darkness whose phenomena the whole world has to endure with and history has to remember.

Manu had dined with little interest tonight. The liquid served to him as 'mountainous herbal water to keep fever at bay in his physically weak condition' had a queer pungency oozing out of it. He drank a little portion and left for his room swerving under various influences – that of his physical weakness, lack of sleep, mental tiredness... and of course strong liquor. For it was liquor (alcohol)[56] that was served to him that night!

---

[56] The Asuras had a tradition of liquor or alcohol consumption among women folk too – a trait that was exclusively associated with Asur society in Vedic times.

A delirious Manav King lay in silence in his chamber. It was illuminated by a small fire glowing lazily in a grate kept in corner to keep the room warm. He wasn't asleep when a few minutes after he saw Ira enter in. She wore a crimson dress which framed her form exquisitely… delivering a daunting effect coupled with the fiery colours flung by the flame.

She strode oddly… strangely smiling, inviting.

Coming up-to him Ira sat on the bed by his side. Manu gazed motionlessly as if in a trance when her hands clutched his hand…

"Shubhe!" he got up fighting his delirium defying her clasp, "you…you shouldn't be here."

"But why?" she respired, "Why can't I be here with you... why won't you look into my eyes once…" the girl implored.

The man stood and staggered – looking at her. He beheld an eager maiden there in her face…driven by desire. Her eyes were appealing, miens were inviting…

Despite not being in absolute charge Manu turned with a jerk and swayed aside. He motioned to leave the room when Ira uttered,

"I leave. Do not trouble yourself… you stay here." And she walked out of the chamber much to the relief of her perturbed hostage.

III

That same night it could be around the mid-hour.

Manu wasn't able to sleep sound due to the disturbing goings-on he had encountered an hour ago. His awareness lay awake, but the faculties slumbered…effects of the strong wine were working. He resisted rest, trying to think over the strange sequences of the past months which 'must be linked somehow – but how'? Discerning so he must have finally slept… for he then saw a dream…

He dreamt -

A maiden fair 'n white

Descended into that night

As an elusive reverie

Quivering like petals sundry

Dressed in a pale wrap

A flawless white trap

Her forehead bore a dot

That scarlet hypnotic spot

She walked carved out of light

The maiden fair 'n white

Descending into that night!

Manu sat up in his bed. The fire in the room was exhausted and it was dark save for the shallow moonlight entering from a small window slit. The figurine in white smiled,

"…Aaryaputra!"

"…I know you! …I… I know you certainly…" enticed, Manu rose

"Aarya Manu…!"

He stepped up eagerly, "….Manu!" said he, "Yes I know that name! You…you are… Oh… I can't remember! But I know you!"

"Yes you know me…and you love me. You must remember me Aarya Manu, you love me," she was sailing closer.

"Y…yes…I think…"

"Remember these white flowers, do they remind you of a day when you…"

"Yes…yes they do…"

IV

Ira woke up early. She prepared to leave before Manu would rise. She dwelled there, looking at his attractive serene face…

She sat lovingly admiring his charming features. Her eyes slid through his affable nose bridge, his glamorous mouth… his obliging chin. They mounted on his broad forehead and rested on his hypnotic, elongated eyes which though concealed currently were still capable of spinning a mystic world around the bemused beholder! They could penetrate through everything, but had failed to see her. Or 'they could see everything but me', thought Ira.

Manu was sleeping like charisma personified. She saw how regally he slept… his face was calm and peaceful maybe for the first time in these three and a half months. His black hair curled mystically over his elegant forehead which Ira daintily rearranged. For the first and probably the only time Manu had let her do this. Life couldn't be kinder.

She must leave now, she knew… And touching her lips to his hand for one last time, she finally emerged out of that wondrous cosmos she had spent her night in.

V

The day advanced and Ira sauntered as if on the seventh heaven, relishing each moment she had been close to the man she loved as dearly as life. She had never been so happy. What an emotion love is, when it is at its peak the rest of the world seems to be a uselessly negligible fraction of subsistence! Not worth even to be attended to.

Ira whiled away the whole day in ecstasy, in remembrance, in anxiety, in anticipation. How was she going to face him from now on? Will he remember anything?

VI

Manu woke up relishing the memory of a fantastic dream he had that night…a reverie through which he thought he had travelled into his elusive past. He was up very late that day owing to the various effects that odd night had shown up.

He had risen cheerful and relaxed in the morning as he thought he had a fascinating re-union in his dreams with someone he had known… long cherished, and loved. Obviously his mind could not wade through the distinction between reality and delusion. And this jumble up was the ill-serving side-effect of administering strong liquor to a person who had never had it earlier.

The day progressed and the intense thinker[57] Manu was able to subtly reconcile with certain sequences of yesterday night's events. He had remembered, how Ira had entered his room in a very… a very inappropriate rather suggestive fashion. He was shaken at the idea. Ira…?

He had trusted her as a friend who had done so much for him – tended to him in a situation when he had been totally dependent on her as a feeble and helpless stranger. He had always seen her as a girl with a kind heart and lively nature. He considered the Princess Ira of Causeruman as someone who held affability and optimism as her adjectives… with a childish exuberance around her which he rather liked. Nothing more, nothing less.

But if she had been harbouring such... clumsy feelings for him (which was evident that she was) he must prevent her immediately. Because he knew he did

[57] Manu – meaning the intense thinker (derived from Manan - means 'to think' in Sanskrit)

not love her. He could not. His diminished but alive memory had time and again told him that his heart was already infused with the sentiment of love lavishly…

And it wasn't for her. He could not let Ira live with it when he knew how painful it would end up being for her. Manu felt an urgency to refrain Ira from advancing any further on the road which was blocked. But how to talk to her?

The evening duly arrived. Manu evaded Ira since morning as even she was reluctant. She was straying on some cloud of her self-created heaven which probably never even existed. She was happy, but also curious to know - now what?

Keeping her secret sojourn only to herself she had not spoken to anyone about it. Not even to Nadia. She was waiting to see Manu first. She needed to see him once before... Nadia would wait Ira knew.

Manu came to his room quite late in the evening. He had spent the day whiling away time in the bare barren vicinity of their highly perched abode. Refusing the supper he had sufficed with a few dried fruits and honey.

Ira approached his room slowly… entered in apprehensively, neurotically shifting her gaze from floor to his face. The greatest King of first Manavas was equally nervous. He couldn't think of a way to initiate the dialogue after that strange behaviour of his 'friend'. However with a slight difficulty he said,

"Shubhe, I pray you… you should not have come here at this hour. I know it is rude the way I behave with you, but I feel …"

Ira gaped quiet. Like a statue… With despondent eyes about to overspill…

"I must tell you that I know… At least I think … Oh! I know…" he tried again.

"What… do you know Aarya?" tears had come rolling,

"It…it isn't you Shubhe,"

"And? Can it never be me as well..?"

"….." he lowered his eyes.

Ira walked out of the room for the last time. Defeated, glum, but resolute. She was coming out of a wonder-world where one knows there will be no entry ever again.

She then cried for her heart – wept for the whole night.

Whatever she had expected her devious arrangement to bring to her she did not seriously think. Obviously it never crossed her mind that it was going to be as miserable as this… A downright rejection of any acknowledgement from the man she had spent the night with. But then how well did she know such matters? Or how well did she know Manu?

VII

The few conical pine trees planted around the cottage stood tall piercing the skies in front of Ira. They looked sardonically linear, as if reinstating the need to see straight ahead of you – which she did not.

She sat basking in the faint sunlight on a carved rock seat outside her cottage the next evening at Brazant Giri. Her countenance was sullen and her eyes were swollen.

It was more than a week since Ira, Manu and Nadia had been residing at this remotely secluded resort. The frost fallen during the previous week still covered the whole setting in an unblemished lightness, enunciating the beauty of everything that is fair and white as was bestowed to the world. It was in stark contrast with the compassions Ira's heart had held till date. And she was able to see the anomaly in full light now…

She had cheated, made Manu love her, got him involved through a heartless trickery. Spending the night in the arms of a flummoxed Manav King in his room Ira had forgotten the why's, what's and how's of her passionate actions and their momentary remunerations.

"It is alright Ira… we are all ordinary people. And we do make mistakes," Nadia walked up closer stroking her golden head softly. She had been watching her quietly since the previous morning, seeing her travel through a range of divergent tangents. She had not disturbed the drive, she knew Ira needed to introspect.

Princess Ira had unmindfully indulged into or rather thrown herself into a serious mess that one night when she asked for wine, white flowers and a white wrap – the dress-up of Kamayani. Nadia knew what she was intending to do.

It wasn't wise…it could not be wise. Ira had designed a ploy that was going to be disastrous for sure! Because men like Manu can never be won through physical attractions. Patience and perseverance could have paid off some day… but! For this love-struck maiden each credo had proved much far-fetched.

Two mornings had dawned since. Manu was not visible around anywhere during the daytime, and with Ira staying indoors Nadia was patiently waiting for the intensity of her hard twirled emotions to settle down. Ira had eluded any colloquy which Nadia respected. By the second evening the Asur Princess seemed finally through with her inner tussling. She had emerged out of her room to sit in the fresh, cool air. She would be able to converse now, judged Nadia.

Ira lifted her head and Nadia looked into her blue eyes – big round eyes that were burdened and blackened with dark circles around. Her cheeks were drained of colour… the face-contours seemed to have withered away. Nadia saw she suddenly looked matured.

"Nadia, he does not love me. He never will. I was a fool not to understand this! You know, I now realize how deep the sentiment of love takes its seat…. into his heart, into my core, into anyone's soul in this big great world. It…it is so true, so genuine that no intrusion can alter it Nadia! I know now… that love has more brilliance than the bright shining sun. There is no cloud that can cover it even momentarily. Love, Nadia, is real…. it is bound to reflect through the layers. I…I have learnt this lesson the harder way, the wrong way."

Nadia listened.

"I had thought," Ira continued, "that he will forget his Kamayani if he loses his memory. But not for a single second, Nadia trust me… not for a minute she has been away from him. She has occupied his senses and her glimpses have illuminated his seclusions ever since he came here. Oh! I…I could have never imagined it to be so beautiful, Nadia!"

"You… what happened that night? Tell me, Ira… if you feel okay,"

"I am. I am okay for the first time probably my good Nadia. Do not go by these tears, (wiping her tears) they are worth the remorse… I do not say that I repent doing what I did. I still believe I could do nothing else.

Nadia, I have loved Aarya Manu with all that I had in me. And I will love him till I breathe my last on this earth. But then maybe, I could not be reciprocated… didn't deserve to have him love me. I see this very clearly Nadia, I really can not deserve to have him. How could I… I've never known the sanctity which exists in every emotion, or each sentiment that prevails across the reign of heart. I could not see the truth!" she paused.

"But I see it now... Now when I've gained so much and lost so much in one single night. Nadia, Aarya Manu gave a meaning to my life when he held me in his arms... and I lost the right to be loved by him when I deceived him.

Nay... I will not die without him, I will live now. Because this... this essence of true love is going to make me live. You know, I've seen... I've understood. I know my good Nadia... I know that love gives you a sacred strength... a zeal which sublimes into your conscious... it becomes the core of your existence. Love never kills – it is the lust that kills! Nadia, oh my good Nadia! How I faltered!" Ira broke down once again and finding solace in her friend's comforting embrace relieved herself of all that had been weighing upon her gentle, pressed soul.

She told her the sequence of events that had happened on that fateful night at Brazant Giri. Nadia listened quietly with continuous tears squirming out of her small un-blinking eyes...

The two girls bared their hearts to each other. The night they were talking about wasn't ordinary... It was going to play an important part in shaping up the Manava's future one day.

SECTION IV

AFTER HER LOVE STORY

CHAPTER 20
AT THE STONE-CASTLE

I

Nadia was reading out a letter to Ira from her father, "... and your Noah's people Manavas have reached our outpost at Banasur's cantonment. The twelve Adityas led by mighty Shakra himself are marching alongside them. The whole army will most probably reach there by another 3-4 days. We have received drum signals[58] sent by our men posted at Bana's base. I was expecting this, but not so early. Now I am preparing to hand over their man back to them and therefore you must return immediately here to the castle. Any further concession in this regard is not allowed to you my dear child, so come at once."

The abiding crew wound up quickly to return at their King's orders.

II

Everything had changed in a fortnight. Ira, Manu, Banasur and King Shambar's lives had changed completely, irreversibly and forever unexpectedly.

Ira was transformed... From being a wilful, carefree Asur princes she had translated into a mature girl

---

[58] a primitive way of conveying messages wherein drum beats were used to transmit coded messages

apprehending the musings of a sacred emotion called love.

The strange night at Brazant Giri had reinstated Manu's belief in himself once again. He had gained the re-assurance of his past and a certainty of its presence which will lead him to regain his lost memory ultimately. But there was a strange pang – a devout suspicion of having submitted to a wrong zone sometime during his stay at the Brazant Giri. It had to do something with the night he had seen two people enter his room and his thoughts. Ira and…? And a hallucination?

Banasur had lost everything and every hope yet again to Manu, his deplorable repetitive offender. Ousted from the mainstream kingdom he was now busy creating some insubstantial line of attack, erecting another stone hedge at the outskirts of Causeruman territory which ultimately proved too fragile to defend his life.

Shambar had lost his peace of mind and his beloved daughter's smile – the most precious thing for him in the world. He was also almost on the verge of losing his people's lives and his kingdom.

III

The Asuras at the castle were wearily waiting a further news from Banasur. Then one day it came…

Banasur, the obstinate Asur chief commandant had revolted. He had overridden his King's orders that were to be diplomatic and peaceable. His amassed anger against the Manavas drove him into thinking that he could be a match for their (Manava's) out of practice combative team which of late (as far as he knew) had been reluctant to display any aggression[59]. Quite idiotically!

Badgering upon his anger as his principal armament Banasur had gone on to wage a war against the Adityas and the Manav fraternity who had reached his post searching for their culprits at Causeruman. The foolhardy Banasur fought against the well-prepared league with a handful of Asur men by his side... obviously with a predictable result.

He lost the battle and his worthless life equally futilely at the hands of a highly infuriated Aditya leader Shakra in no time. The remaining Asuras (who-so-ever survived) pleaded for their lives and were granted bail by the judicious Shakra. Taking directional cues from them the rescue army (Manavas + Adiyas) advanced towards their next target, Shambar's stone castle where their precious Manu was kept confined.

For Shambarasur the loss of his chief commander Banasur wasn't as worrisome as was the ire of the approaching warriors. They had to be pacified. Shambar had known his opponents and their might so well since earlier times – who didn't know the Vasus, the Marutas, (now collectively known as Manavas) or the Adityas!

---

[59] Book ref. 'From Zero To One – the story of Manu' by MVG (Maneesha Agrawal)

IV

Grey skies thundered under a cloudy disguise at Causeruman. The Aditya-Asur battles were always considered ominous. Scores of lives were lost and tons of assets were ruined. The Asuras had wasted their lives on account of their foolish recklessness so many times that they were already on the verge of extinction, the Great Floods[60] adding to the damages. Shambar could not risk yet another dissipation of this only residual Asur civilization.

The Asur King Shambarasur stood on the roof-top of his stone citadel looking at the obdurate stone hedge. His eyes rested on the unyielding bastions of his castle. They were impervious structures and they appeared invincible. But what were they, in front of Shakra's stone-crushing Vajra[61]? And what were they, as compared to Vayu[62] and Pawan[63]'s indomitable Chakras[64]? Or Prithu's or Poosha's famous Mallet? Or Agni's never failing fierce missiles? This stone hedge will be merely a mound he knew.

Even if the Asuras stayed inside their protected fortress, the Adityas were known to force their way into the opponent's territory through some unthinkable dexterity. Shambar had seen it happen at the earlier battles (with Madasur). Weighing his own strength vis-à-vis the rivals, Shambarasur knew his trepidations.

---

[60] Book ref. 'From Zero To One – the story of Manu' by MVG (Maneesha Agrawal)

[61] A deadly weapon used by the Aditya leader which was known to be unassailable if used.

[62] The Maruta's commanders (now Manavas)

[63] The Maruta's commanders (now Manavas)

[64] A multi-edged weapon which could crush any opposition

If they fought this absolutely avoidable feud, the already receding Asuras could be left at struggling to reach beyond a double figure in numbers even if they survived the battle. What a waste it would be… when all this could and should be handled with some tact.

All these considerations made Shambar to think with a cool head so unlike of him and his tribe. But for the sake of his tribe only he could not make his people pay heavily with their lives on account of a stupid infatuation his daughter had leapt into.

A dialogue will have to be chartered very carefully… the son of King Surya wasn't any mundane figure to get kidnapped without serious repercussions.

Shambar called Nadia, Damas and two of his other worthy counsel in his private chamber. They held a detailed discussion on every possible aspect of the given situation for long hours. The extensive meeting ended at reaching upon a few deliberations. Following it Nadia approached Ira in her room,

"We are going to return Aarya Manu." she said, "In a few minutes from now. I, Damas and your father the King are travelling to take him to the Manavas. We are left without a choice after what Banasur has done. Unless we take Aarya Manu immediately away from here there is every possibility that we get embroiled in a worse… frankly a sort of more complex situation. There is also the risk that you will be called to answer a few gruelling questions… which we do not want. So looking at the situation we have decided ….Ira? Are you listening to what I say?"

Ira looked back at her with blank vacant eyes, "Yes. I heard you. You said you are going to take Aarya Manu away back to the Manavas, back to Kamayani and to the Himalayas.... To Manali the place where he belongs. This is the right thing.... take him away. Let him go. He must go. And he must be happy... always... happy with his people, his Kamayani, and his homeland. Me, I do not figure... I am... I'm no-one to him... and will never be. But I'll live Nadia.... I will. Live without him... oh yes I will live..."

Nadia's small intelligent eyes glistened quietly as she asked the Princess if she would want to see or speak to Manu for a one last time. Ira shook her golden head in refusal.

CHAPTER 21
THE REUNION

I

After eliminating Banasur easily Shakra and rest of the crusaders were hurrying through the peripheries of Causeruman kingdom. They knew they were on the right track. Their ire had already increased multi-fold at the Asur camp's unrepentant audacity. After kidnapping their precious Manu treacherously they had shown the guts to fight? Outrageous!

The agitated army's robust horses were stomping the environs of Causeruman like an approaching thunderclap now. And to talk of the riders, they were fuming like fireballs!

Suddenly Dhata and Savita the two forerunner riders and the troupe's adroit explorers called for a halt. They were signalling the group to stop - holding their hands up they shouted,

"Aarya Shakra, look…!"

"…what is it Dhata?"

"It is Aarya Manu. I can see him coming with a few Asur riders… they are visible at a distance over there..."

The campaigners slowed. They could also see some people coming along with Manu among them.

Shakra, Prithu, Vaayu and other prominent members of the troupe waited anxiously to understand. They were armed and prepared for their unexpected greeters (Asuras) to receive them the way they would. But there wasn't seen any army!

Then what of Manu?? Was he captive… chained?

No. They saw clearly that he was riding free of any fastening. Surprising. Why wasn't he hurrying up to them? Something was weird… amiss. They were perplexed!

"Namaskar[65] Aarya Shakra." Greeted Shambarasur as he came forward leading a small troupe of just five members, "and greetings to all the other members of the Aditya and Manav community. I welcome you all to my peaceful kingdom of Causeruman. I believe you all have been travelling from quite a distance Aaryagana[66]. I invite you to be our guests at the…"

"Greetings Shambarasur. We are not here to be your guests," roared Shakra, "What we want first is the whole story from you… right now, right here!" he had already appreciated the lack of a military preparation from the other side.

"Aarya Shakra, I am here for that only. But first let me submit to you the fact that we have come here with your esteemed leader Manu who is, as you can see for yourself not in a very healthy state. Can we for his sake,

---

[65] A way of greeting, welcome with folded hands

[66] Aarya people in plural (aarya + gana = aarya + people)

assemble amicably in the cantonment vacated by Banasur nearby?"

The much surprised Adityas and Manavas saw Shambarasur was accompanied by a plain looking girl, and only three of his unarmed men apart from Manu. Then Manu… why, something was the matter with him. He was much paler and thinner – yes, that was there. But his face, his expressions?

Manu did not register a recognition to his own people. How? …why? He was looking at them with a bright, lit up face… apparently optimistic to reach out to them… But why on earth did he not recognize or greet them - Shakra, Prithu, Som, Vaayu… no one?

II

Seated amidst the scarce comforts of cantonment at the Causeruman outpost Shambar went on to explain the complete story aided by Nadia and Damas.

The Adityas were told, how a venomous scorpion had stung Manu that day making him susceptible to being poisoned. Then how Damas had found him about to collapse, fidgeting in pain by the riverbed that evening and helped him to their campsite. They had nursed him with the available anti-dote. But then they all had panicked seeing the sting working very fast.

They told in a bid to save his life their Princess had immediately carried him to Causeruman where proper medication for the sting was available… in the fright forgetting to inform his people the Manavas.

The assemblage were told how their Princess Ira had tended the ailing Manav King when he had started losing his memory as an after-effect of the poison and its anti-dote. "But the effect does not last beyond at the most five-six months, that is two more months from now maximum… and Aarya Manu will regain everything he's lost," Damas had elucidated noticing stern glares from the listeners.

Then Shambar recounted how they had announced him the 'Heir to the throne and Ira's future husband' in a bid to cover up his antecedents – he was son of Surya and Shakra both of whom were widely known as staunch enemies of Asuras ever since earlier times.

"Any of my own men could have killed you knowing the truth about you… had it not been for Ira's insistence to cover your identity. We were committed to take you back to your own place once you were in a better physical and mental health," Shambar had explained turning to Manu.

"We even decided to call you with a different name, Noah - for the same risk… of someone identifying you with your more famously known name, Aarya Manu," added Nadia.

Whether they were convinced or not, it is a detail which no one ought to be interested in really knowing, one has to think. Because at the end of it the Manavas had their precious leader safe with them and they were taking him back to his own people and place. And Shambarasur and his men must have heaved a sigh at the mercifully uneventful departure of the heavenly crusaders - they all had left Causeruman without a display of any resentment. Their chief commander was the Asura's only casualty but it will surely be made up for pretty soon! They could certainly do without Banasur.

That is how the whole episode finally ended. Well, still not quite, maybe.

CHAPTER 22

AFTER A YEAR

I

Kamayani was serenely watching her first born son Ikshvaku in her own backyard at Manali.

The Manavas had recently discovered a stem of a plant they called 'Ikshu' (Sanskrit term for Sugarcane) from which a very sweet tasting juice could be extracted. It was a useful discovery. To commemorate this chance finding of 'Ikshu' the Manavas had honoured it with naming their leader's first born child 'Ikshvaku' after it since both had arrived almost together in their society to sweeten their lives.

Kamayani was sitting under a fir tree amidst rows of wild flowers blooming at the advent of summer season in the cold heights of village Manali.

It was late in the evening. Soon the sun would be rolling over to the other side of Himalayas leaving their village sleep under darkness until resurgence of a new dawn tomorrow. A two month old Ikshvaku lay peacefully in his mother's lap, slumbering in the fading warmth of a sinking sun.

Kamayani saw Manu approaching… his stately stride bedecked with a rubicund effect the rays of a setting sun produced. His form was etched clearly, as if framed by the meticulous sculptor – the Sun God with the interminable rays as his hands. She looked at her husband with loving eyes…

But his face was tensed. He looked pensive and thoughtful. He had held out a letter to her when her eyes questioned him…

"**Letter to the Manav King Aarya Manu from Princess Ira of Causeruman**.

Greetings to Aarya Manu, Namaskar.

I am Ira. I am a culprit who has escaped sentence for all my misdoings from the illustrious Manavas, Adityas and even the usually unpretentious Asuras. It has happened because no one except for me, Nadia, my father and now my would-be husband Damanasur know the real story that has unfolded during the last one and a half year. No one knows, because everything was concealed… in a spurious grab for the fear of injuring many important lives more gravely than death.

But now the time has come Aarya Manu, for it to be confessed and disclosed to you and your Kamayani.

Today when I look back at it, I know and I realize how impossible I have made it to be believed! The Ira you will know from today onwards is a sly Asur girl, who recognizes nothing but her insatiable desire to own and acquire. In the process forfeiting all the morals of sanctified social living. The way I've conceived and connived… beginning from your heavenly village Manali and stretching to this far off Kingdom of Causeruman… I have been spiralling a highly preposterous yarn of perjury, deceit and decadence…. you must know it now. If I still keep it from you I would be forever guilty of a greater debauchery.

It all started on the day when I first saw you on the banks of Arjikiya…"

The letter went on to explain every single detail of whatever had happened at Manali. How the Princess fell for Manu, and how she stooped lower step after step each day - planning and plotting to win him over.

Manu was firstly appalled at the disclosures. But progressing through it he was able to see the immature young girl that Ira actually was. He could not come to blame her.

He had brought the letter straight to Kamayani. She read through the lines quietly, initially in the horror of the unthinkable tale the text was unfolding in each paragraph. She saw the desperation unkempt love can beget, as she read the scandalous episode enacted upon that one night at Brazant Giri. The letter said,

"…..that one night gave me.

Aarya Manu, it was and shall always be the only worth my futile life can ever boast of. And it has borne me a treasure which is inimitable but not earned by me deservedly.

I righteously believe that I have no moral right to keep it with me so I am returning it to you. It belongs to you and Kamayani. This is my attempt at connecting with you for a final and one last time. Forgive me Aarya Manu, if you can… this is one hope that I can live in the light of. And forget those follies committed by a very young, immature, obstinate Asur girl.

With a wish never to make you hear from me ever in this life, and yet aspiring to be with you (maybe even deserve you) sometime in some other heaven,

Forgettable,

Ira.

To Kamayani

Greetings to the Manav Queen.

I could never have written to you even with all my courage gathered in my fingers. But I am writing to you trusting your kindness as I've known you possess through your distinguished husband.

Kamayani, I have committed gross injustice not only to the trust, affection and warmth I received from you and your people... I am also guilty of carrying it too far – far beyond the limits of conduct befitting a woman. When I made your blameless husband hold me in his arms deceiving him in your grab, I did not realize. But I know now... I know how I've traversed my own decency. I want to tell you today everything about the complete episode, for you need to know that not even for one single second he's been away from you.

I could not differentiate what was driving me mad... was it lust or love. But at least today I see where real love is borne in a loving heart..."

The letter explained every emotion Ira had been through that day and later - after the night at Brazant Giri.

It had opened up every section of Ira's heart, to the extent that her readers (Manu & Kamayani) were able to actually visualise the sufferings of her heart which had driven her unethical. They could see the anguish, the misery love can bring to an immature, 'out of bound' heart which had never known the frenzy of such a strong emotion.

The letter was an admittance on how a delicate feeling can lose its beauty and charm if it starts churning the wrong corners of mind rather than the heart. The sore can, if left unattended, escalate into an abscess for not only one person... but would inflict pain to the whole set-up of a civilization.

The Manav and the Asur civilizations had come nearly on the verge of eliminating each other following the selfish misdeeds carried out by the two desperate girls driven by uncontrolled desire. Ira's love for Manu and Nadia's sentiment for Ira couldn't see this wisdom. Nevertheless, right lessons were learnt at just about the right time.

Ira had learnt the accuracy of being human shedding her Asur instincts,

".....and so finally I've acceded to marry our good Damas at the behest of my Father.

But this child belongs to you Kamayani... it was you whom your husband thought he was getting close to that night. I can clearly see that I have no moral right to have this baby… She is your and Aarya Manu's child borne by me.

Ira never existed – and you Kamayani, you've never ceased to exist. Not in his dreams, not in his seclusions, not in his delusions… he's never been away from you. The way I have seen him love you, I shall pray to the Lord Almighty that he makes every girl under the sun be loved like this. May Aarya Manu and his Kamayani stay together… always and forever".

Kamayani looked into the eyes of her husband. Both the pairs were dampened.

"Aaryaputra, will you judge her for whatever she did or… or maybe she had to do?" Kamayani asked Manu.

"No one Kamayani, has the right to judge anyone other than oneself." said he resolutely, "because whatever one does…or one has to do, must come around to self only."

"But you don't think she's liable to be subjected to continuous suffering because of her immature understanding of love… do you? She must still be in love with you only. Marrying someone else whom she did not love, and never being able to see you or her own borne child! It is going to be another constant, endless suffering for her."

"Every life has a story which gives accountability to the way it was lead. This is a domain where everything comes equal in the end – the morals, ethics, norms or whatever codes we observe as right or wrong are nothing but the equations to solve and settle life's accountability. Such simple are the accounts of our lives.

We are social beings Kamayani. We are a population with certain civil responsibilities that require discipline. So there is an obvious need to have the demarcations of rights and wrongs. But I would say that before employing them to the society, we have to employ them individually to our own conduct. Because in employing these rights and wrongs to ourselves lie the privilege of being a human being – the creator's best creation.

Each one of us must remember that we are civil, evolved out from the crudity and ferocity of desires, emotions, hunger, lust and wants. They are the traits that are meant to be treated and controlled as traits; not to be pursued as goals. Otherwise how do we distinguish ourselves from savage cavemen or unrefined brutes who hurt and kill to satiate their hunger? They cannot be called fit for social living!

Desire, dreams, love, longing…all are such adorable emotions that emerge to make living beautiful and worthwhile. But they have to be reined in … driven towards being constructive, being helpful to carve smiles out of stones. Turn them into some fervour that coaxes hurling stones, they will lead to the contemptable degeneration of a lovely life… and sometimes a complete civilization."

"But then Aaryaputra, we are merely human. We cannot be always divine and grand, and perfect in emotions. Sometimes we falter. Out of adolescence or puerility I should say, not because of viciousness. They ought to be forgiven then…?"

"True. We err. And must be forgiven. But first by our own selves. If I am able to forgive myself, then only I can expect an apology from my society or people around me whom I've wronged. This is the rule that I believe in."

"So…?"

"…Umm?"

"So you will forgive Ira and her friend Nadia?"

"I…well, I shall never judge Ira or her friend Nadia. Or anyone else involved in the whole sequence. I can see that she's undergone her share of sufferings already. She may have wronged many people in her obsession, and all of them have regained everything they had lost – but for her.

The Causeruman Princess is the one who has lost her pleasure of living, suffocated under a guilt which is going to make her coming days miserable. This is no less penalty she has to pay all through her life. And we know she has a generous and a genuine heart. That is why she's been able to judge her own deeds and see through the retribution she has decided for herself – staying away from her own child and the… the… love of her life, forever.

Ira is trying to forgive herself - which I am sure she will ultimately achieve after serving her time. This should suffice for her. In fact as I look at it, she is her own culprit in the first place. Where is then, the need for me or you to arbitrate her actions?"

Kamayani held her husband in higher esteem today. Her fears of Manu having unpleasant feelings for Ira were now abated. She had liked Ira and felt sympathetic for the hapless girl... After all, Manu was capable of inducing such charm.

She remembered her days when she had fallen for this adorable man... and how severely it had hurt[67] her. What could the poor girl do to curb such a draw! She felt sorry for the star-crossed Asur Princess. She quietly studied Manu's face – it was calm and composed now. The storm that had crossed Manali and the Manavas a year and a half ago had finally subsided.

"Where is the child?" she asked.

"Inside", he said.

The couple lifted their still sleeping Ikshvaku and entered their chalet. There Kamayani saw, wrapped up in a white stole with golden borders (it was Manu's stole which he had left at Causeruman) lay a beautiful child... a five month old girl with curled ringlets of golden hair circling her divine, smiling face. She waved her tiny white hands at the Manav Queen calling out,

"....da!"

Kamayani looked at her twinkling blue eyes, then back at her husband and said,

---

[67] Book Ref : 'From Zero To One – The Story Of Manu' by MVG (Maneesha Agrawal)

"Yes. She is mine…and yours. Our Illa."

Manu nodded.

CULMINATION – AFTERWORD

This is a story which is a prelude to the widespread history of Indian sub-continent. Manushyas, or the Manavas are believed to be the followers of the first King Shradhhdev Manu son of King Surya, whose wife is known to be Kamayani (or Shraddha at some places) in ancient Sanskrit texts.

Their first born child was Ikshvaku who became the celebrated ancestor of the very famous Suryavansh (namely King Surya's descendants). He is credited with commencing a legacy which earned greater respect years later by being the acclaimed dynasty in which Lord Rama was born. Suryavanshi (the one born in Surya dynasty) Lord Rama is the most famous descendant of the bequest established by Manu at the beginning of this current ongoing eon[68].

The child borne by Ida or Ira, as mentioned in the available old texts (the Puranas which are great sources of our history) is believed to be a girl named Illa or Ella. She is stated to be brought up by Kamayani and Manu, and there's no mention of what became of her biological mother Ira.

Ira is mentioned as someone who had loved and led Manu astray to some undisclosed region, for an unknown time. She had mislead the Manav King somehow deviating him from his decided path, but had realized and rectified her mistake ultimately by leaving

---

[68] Book ref. 'From Zero To One – the story of Manu' by MVG (Maneesha Agrawal)

Manu and her new born child soon after her birth. She had disappeared never to surface again. These are the only available outlines of the story as found in our ancient texts.

The girl Illa or Ella had married Budh, son of Som or Chandra (a close aide to Manu) who was originally a Vasu[69]. Chandra is actually the more widely popular name of Som.

Manu's daughter Ella and Budh gave birth to Pururava, the renowned fore-bearer of the Chandravansh or Chandra dynasty, in which the Pandavas (of Mahabharata fame) were born. King Pururava earns his reputation as the mortal human being who had troubled the heavens in order to marry Urvashi who was a celestial entity. She was an Apsara (a divine beauty) who fell in love with King Pururava. He is the only king known in the ancient texts who went on to succeed in bringing an Apsara down to earth.

Having briefly explained how the Surya-vansh and the Chandra-vansh both originated from one person Manu, I think I have been able to create a connection for my reader. This is the pattern our history has found its way through...starting from Manu, branching out further into sub-dynasties and categories, expanding in to more diversified rulers of the ancient and medieval age, and finally all those monarch dynasties dissolving into the Cosmopolitan, Global population of the current modern India.

---

[69] One of the Vedic divine clans (Rudras, Adityas, Vasus, Marutas, Gandharvas, Yakshas, Humans) their seniority being in descending order. See for ref. 'From Zero To One - the story of Manu' by MVG (Maneesha Agrawal)

In whichever way we may remember or forget Manu we cannot scrap away the fact that the scientific researches of today have strongly indicated a common gene pool for us. Majority of the races, caste and creed of us human beings that are currently sharing space are found to be genetically close to one another.

Although results of such researches are yet to be authenticated, but it definitely yields a plausible truth – we were born close and flourished unified someday. The unnecessary divisions that we've come to practicing today appear all the more absurd in this light.

How interesting it is therefore, to think that once upon a time we may have been living together as one single society under the same crest. To imagine that even today we are linked together through some distant blood relations surpassing the vast boundaries of land, region or culture… Delightful, isn't it!